WORTH THE WAIT

CINDY KIRK

D1736190

WAVERLY
HOUSE

ISBN: 9798668317226

First published in 2007 as ROMANCING THE NANNY by Silhouette Books

CHAPTER ONE

It was lust, Amy Logan decided as she pressed the dough into the pie crust with extra fervor. Pure and simple lust.

After all, it would be unnatural to live with such a handsome man for three years and not have the occasional urge to see him naked.

Having no sex in years probably didn't help either, Amy thought, her lips twisting upward in a wry smile. Or the fact that this morning she'd slipped upstairs to get Emma her backpack and caught him just out of the shower.

Oh, he'd been perfectly presentable with a Turkish towel wrapped firmly around his waist. She'd certainly seen him with his shirt off before.

Every summer he went to the pool at the country club with her and Emma at least a couple of times.

But there was something different about knowing that he'd been naked only moments before. Something about seeing the droplets of water clinging to his broad chest. Something about smelling that delicious mixture of soap, shampoo and clean masculine flesh.

Amy inhaled deeply. Even now if she closed her eyes, she could still—

"Got any coffee left?"

Amy's eyes popped open and she stilled, grateful she faced the wall. Otherwise the object of her desires might think she was having a sensual experience with a pie crust.

Schooling her features into what she hoped was a nonchalant expression, Amy turned.

Dan Major stood in the center of the large modern kitchen wearing her favorite suit. The cut emphasized his broad shoulders and lean hips and the navy color brought out the brilliant blue of his eyes. Still damp from the shower, his short dark hair fell into a careless wave on his forehead.

He was an inch or two over six feet and easily the most handsome man she'd ever known. It only made sense that she'd want to see him naked. What didn't make sense was why that desire had taken so long to surface.

She and the hunky widower had lived side by side for almost three years. Amy had always considered Dan a good friend. But over the past six months she'd found herself thinking of him in a different way, seeing him not just as her employer and friend but as a desirable man.

"Amy?"

His lips curved upward and she realized with a start that she'd been staring.

Without a word, she reached over and lifted the pot from the warmer. "Can I pour you a cup?"

"You don't have to always get my coffee," he protested as he pulled out a chair and took a seat at the table.

Amy smiled. Dan was the quintessential modern man with one major exception. Despite being only thirty-four and having been raised in a progressive two- income family, Dan rarely helped out around the house.

She had only herself to blame. She'd refused his offers of help so many times, he'd quit asking. Even though it was her job, she enjoyed knowing he didn't have to worry about the house or meals and could focus his free time being with his daughter.

A successful architect at one of Chicago's largest and most prestigious firms, Dan alternated between working in the office or from home.

His schedule was so varied, Amy never knew if he'd be home, at the office, or out meeting with clients. It didn't really affect her. Emma was in first grade this year and gone all day. The only difference was, if Dan was home she'd make his lunch and maybe offer a snack in the afternoon.

After all, that's what he was paying her for; that and taking care of his young daughter, Emma. Not only did he pay her, he paid her very well. With the extra money she saved by living-in, she'd been able to get enough cash together to start a small catering business.

Last year when she'd shown Dan her business plan he'd been supportive, but concerned she would leave. She'd reassured him that this was just something extra she wanted to do for herself.

Shortly after that he'd had the antiquated kitchen in the large older home remodeled. Best of all, he'd solicited her input and hadn't batted an eye at her request for commercial-grade appliances.

For now she limited her efforts to catering small parties on the weekends and providing specialty desserts to a couple of restaurants. But she held high hopes for the future. One day she'd make enough so she could have her own home—

"I'd be happy to get my own coffee..."

Dan's bemused voice broke through her reverie pulling Amy back to the present. She glanced down at the coffeepot she still held loosely in her hand. Ignoring Dan's teasing comment, Amy quickly poured a cup and set the steaming brew in front of him.

"Cinnamon roll?" she asked, appealing to his sweet tooth. "I made them this morning. Or I could whip up some bacon and eggs? It would only take a second—"

"I'm afraid this will have to do." Dan glanced at the clock on the wall, took a hasty sip of coffee and pushed back his chair. "I have a meeting at the office at nine and I should've been gone by now."

As he rose from his chair, Amy reached for the travel mug in the cupboard and filled it with the rich Columbian blend that was his favorite.

By the time she was done he was already in the doorway. He turned. "I should be home early, around five-thirty."

Amy let her gaze sweep over him, like it did over Emma every morning, making sure everything was in place. She frowned.

"Wait." She popped the lid on the travel mug and quickly crossed the room. Instead of handing him the coffee, she placed it on the counter and stepped close. "Your tie needs some help."

Grabbing the silk fabric, she loosened the off- center knot and with well-practiced ease and quickly retied it. Instead of taking a step back, she let her fingers linger.

Dan was in a hurry. He'd made that perfectly clear. Her head told her to step back, hand him the travel mug and send him on his way. Her feet wouldn't move. The air surrounding them grew thick. It was as if an invisible web encased them. Time, which had been ticking forward with rhythmic precision, came to an abrupt halt

The subtle scent of his cologne teased her nostrils. Heat emanating from his body washed over her.

She wanted to pull him close and press her lips to his, relieve this tension that had built up inside her. But while Dan liked, admired, and appreciated her, she'd never seen him show any signs of being attracted to her. Any electricity was definitely one-sided.

Amy dropped her hands, placed them on her rounded hips and gave him a once-over. "Now you look presentable."

"Thanks." The dimple in his left cheek flashed. He reached down and picked up the mug she'd placed on the counter. "I appreciate the coffee."

Somehow Amy managed an easy smile. "Anytime."

She stood at the door and watched him get in the car. As he drove off, she lifted her hand and waved goodbye, then took a few steps and collapsed in a nearby chair. What in the world had she been <u>thinking</u>?

Dan wasn't interested in *her*. Even if there was a tiny spark of something between them, there was no way she could compete with Tess Major's memory and come out ahead. Other women had tried and they'd all failed. That's what Amy needed to remember before she did something she'd live to regret.

The smell of warm peach pie filled the large kitchen and Amy smiled as she wiped down the counters. Some women needed fancy clothes or trips to exotic places, but all it took for her to be happy was a neat, orderly kitchen...

"Something smells good in here."

Amy whirled. Dan stood in the doorway to the dining room, a lazy smile on his lips.

"What are you doing home so early?" The minute the words left her mouth Amy wished she could pull them back. She'd made it sound as if he was unwelcome when nothing could be further from the truth.

She always liked to have everything ready and in its place when he came home. But it was only four-thirty and she hadn't expected him for at least an hour. The table wasn't set and Emma was still down the block playing at a friend's house.

"Now that's a warm welcome." Dan smiled and that familiar dimple in his left cheek appeared. "If I didn't know better, I'd think you didn't want me."

His gaze settled on her and she forced herself not to glance away. But it was hard. The intense look in his blue eyes sent a shiver up her spine. 'Tell me something, Amy. Do you ever think of me when I'm not here?"

That same electricity charged the air and Amy moistened her dry lips. She shifted from one foot to the other, not knowing how to answer. This morning he'd looked at her as if he was seeing her for the first time.

This was another first. In all the years she'd worked for Dan, he'd never spoken to her like this before. There had always been a professional boundary that had never been crossed.

"Of course I think of you," she finally managed to stammer.

He smiled and paused as if he expected her to elaborate.

What else could she say? She certainly wasn't about to bare her soul and confess her desire for some skin-to-skin action. Not to mention that her heart had lodged itself in her throat, making speech impossible.

Thankfully Dan didn't press her for more. Instead he crossed the room, flung his suit jacket over a chair and loosened his tie.

Amy could feel her cheeks warm. She turned back to the counter and scrubbed a nonexistent spot with her sponge.

He stopped directly behind her, so close she could smell the spicy scent of his cologne and feel the heat from his body.

She turned and he was right *there.* Just like this morning it struck her how big he was, how tall. How overwhelmingly male in every way.

Her heart picked up speed.

His gaze lazily appraised her and his eyes darkened. "You're so beautiful."

The compliment rolled from his lips like warm honey. At the end of a busy day, she didn't feel beautiful. The sprinkle of freckles and her 'girl-next-door' looks made her wholesome, rather than beautiful. Under his admiring gaze, for the first time in her twenty-eight years, Amy felt beautiful.

"Thank you."

His lips quirked. "You're very welcome."

Could she be any worse at this flirting stuff? It didn't seem possible.

She started to ask if his meeting had gotten canceled when he took another step forward and his body brushed hers. In that instant Amy forgot how to breathe, much less talk.

With the gentlest of touches, Dan slid his fingers into the warm silky mass at her nape, letting his thumbs graze the soft skin beneath her jaw.

Waves of chills and heat raced through Amy until she was nearly dizzy. He was going to kiss her; she could see it in his eyes. She tossed the sponge to the counter without shifting her gaze from him.

His lips lowered and she let her eyelids drift shut, anticipation coursing through her...

The front door slammed shut.

Amy jumped as if she'd been shot. Panic raced through her. Emma couldn't find the two of them together. She raised a hand to push Dan away and found only air.

Her gaze darted around the room and after a long second it finally sank in...she was alone. There'd been no Dan and no almost-kiss. Heat rose up her neck. She'd had vivid daydreams before, but never with Dan as the star player.

"Amy, I'm home." Emma's childish voice rang out from the foyer.

"In the kitchen," Amy called back. She rubbed her mouth with the back of her hand. Though it had been only a dream, her lips still tingled.

"Is it 'bout time for dinner?" The petite six-year-old bounded into the kitchen, a streak of dirt on her cheek and a grass stain on one knee. "I'm hungry." Amy couldn't help but smile. Dan often joked that the little girl's stomach was a bottomless pit. Emma could eat and five minutes later be hungry. "Once your father gets home, we'll have dinner, He shouldn't be too late."

Amy opened her arms and the girl ran to her. When Amy had been Emma's age, hugs had been in short supply. She'd vowed when she had children, she'd make sure they knew they were loved.

Amy couldn't imagine anything better than having a family of her own—a husband to love, a child to cherish.

Her arms tightened around Emma. One day she'd be a mother. For now, she had Emma to love.

Emma laid her head against Amy's chest. "I love you."

Tears sprang to Amy's eyes at the child's sincerity. "I love you, too, pumpkin."

Yes, for now this would most definitely do.

CHAPTER TWO

Out of the corner of his eye, Dan Major saw a stylish young woman across the bar and realized he knew her. He smiled and she waved.

"Another Dan fan?" Jake Stanley's lips curved upward. "How in the world do you do it?"

"Stuff it, Jake." Dan grabbed some peanuts from the basket in the center of the table and popped them in his mouth.

Seeing old girlfriends only reinforced why Dan found it hard to date. He liked the companionship but women always seemed to want more. Bree was a perfect example. Though she'd professed to being devoted to a singles' lifestyle, after a couple of months, she'd changed her tune.

Dan sighed and glanced around the bar. Although it was only Thursday night, the place was crowded with women from nearby businesses. He suspected that was why Jake had insisted on coming to this bar.

Looking for love in all the wrong places...

For some reason the words to the vintage song popped into Dan's head. The lyrics didn't fit his life. The last thing Dan was looking for tonight, or any other night, was love.

Jake shot Dan a speculative gaze. "Speaking of Dan fans, how's it going with Miranda?"

"Her name is Melinda." Dan kept his tone deliberately offhand. "We're not seeing each other anymore."

"Let me guess." Jake lifted a finger to his lips and pretended to think. "*You* broke up with *her*."

Dan grabbed another handful of peanuts, strangely irritated by the knowing look in his friend's eyes. "What does it matter who decided to end it? The point is it wasn't working."

"It wasn't working because she wanted more than sex," Jake said conversationally, resting his arms on the table. "Things heat up, you back off."

"You don't know squat." Dan's tone was sharper than he'd intended but it had been hard losing Melinda. Just like Bree, she was a nice woman and he'd enjoyed her company. But he refused to promise more than he could deliver.

Jake placed his drink on the table and lifted his hands. "Whoa, buddy. I wasn't saying there was anything wrong with playing the field—"

Dan ignored the envious look in his friend's eye. The truth was Dan didn't like being on the dating merry-go-round. The longer he was with a woman, the more they seemed to want, the more they seemed to need. He'd yet to find a woman who was content to keep it casual. "I made it clear from the very beginning that I didn't want to get married again. Why is that so hard for women to understand?"

"Because regardless of what they say, they want that ring on their finger." Jake lifted a hand and motioned for the waiter to bring him another drink. "I know you've got this thing against marriage but I think you should reconsider."

Dan took a sip of beer. Jake had it all wrong. He didn't have anything against marriage. He'd loved being married to Tess. From the time he'd first laid eyes on her, he'd known she was the one. When they'd said "I do" he'd happily planned on spending the rest of his life with her. His heart twisted.

"You'd have someone to warm your bed and that little girl of yours would have a mother," Jake continued.

Dan shoved aside his memories and smiled at the thought of his daughter. Of all the things he valued most in his life, his six-year-old topped the list. "Emma is coping with the loss of her mother. Amy takes good care of her."

Amy had been his daughter's nanny for three years and Dan knew she loved Emma as if she were her own. She'd made the house a home for both of them.

"Which is all well and good," Jake said. "Until 'nanny' finds a man and decides to get married and leave you."

Amy wouldn't leave me.

Dan bit back the words, shocked at the strength of emotion the thought evoked. He started to say Amy didn't even date, but stopped himself again. There *had* been one guy recently...

He'd been surprised—stunned would actually be closer to the truth—when Amy had casually mentioned she was going to the movies with someone she'd met at her cooking club. In all the years she'd lived under his roof, Dan couldn't remember her dating before. Amy just never seemed like the dating type.

Not that she was ugly or anything. Far from it. With her brown hair, green eyes and a smattering of freckles across her nose, Amy had that natural, all-American look that any man would find attractive. She was smart. While she always had an opinion on the latest current events, she also liked to listen. Any man would be lucky to have her for a girlfriend or wife.

A tightness filled his chest. Jake was right If she left, he'd be stuck. He'd never find another nanny like Amy. He might even have to do what Jake suggested and remarry. A chill traveled up Dan's spine.

Since he'd been fifteen, Tess had been the only woman Dan

had ever wanted in his life. His wife had been beautiful, smart and a rising star in the fashion world with her innovative clothing designs. For the first five years of their marriage, life had been wonderful. Their careers had flourished and the old house they'd purchased in Lincoln Park was perfect for a growing family.

After Emma was born, Tess had decided there would be no more children. She loved her daughter but her pregnancy had been difficult and Emma was a fussy baby. When her new line took off like a skyrocket, her career began demanding more of her time and energy.

Dan had reluctantly put away his dream of a large family, but he hadn't given up completely. When Emma was two he'd convinced Tess to have one more, promising her a full-time nanny. That's when Amy had come to live with them. The second baby he'd wanted so much had died along with Tess.

Guilt washed over him, mixed with an overwhelming sense of loss. He'd give anything to be able to go back and tell Tess he didn't care about having another child or a playmate for Emma, he only cared about having *her* in his life.

"Mark my words, it's going to happen." Jake, appearing to revel in his role as a prophet of doom, pulled Dan back to the present. "It's just a matter of time."

"Amy isn't going to get married." Even if he didn't fully believe them, saying the words out loud made Dan feel better.

She couldn't leave. He depended on her to keep his household running smoothly. He liked having her around. Over the past couple of years they'd become good friends. He couldn't imagine what it would be like if she wasn't there.

"She'll get married." Jake nodded his head to punctuate the point. "I've been thinking about asking her out."

The comment set Dan's teeth on edge. "Forget dating her. I know you too well to let that happen."

Jake just laughed.

"Can I interest you two in some wings?" The waiter leaned across the table and slid Jake's second drink in front of him.

Dan's stomach growled and he realized with a start that lunch had been hours ago. He glanced at his watch and swore. Reaching into his pocket, Dan brought out a couple of bills and tossed them on the table.

"I'll take a plate of the barbecued ones," Jake said to the waiter before shifting his gaze to Dan. He lifted a brow. "You're leaving?"

"I'm late." Dan grabbed his briefcase and rose to his feet. "Amy will have dinner on the table."

"I forgot." Jake sat back in his chair, an inscrutable look on his face. "Superwoman does it all—cleans your house, cares for your kid *and* makes your meals. If you could just get her naked, you'd have it made." Dan ignored the crude comment—and the hint of envy in his friend's tone—and simply smiled.

It was true. Amy had breakfast waiting for him every morning and dinner ready every night. The house was always spotless and, when he entertained, she worked behind the scenes making sure every little detail was covered. Best of all, she cared for Emma as if the child were her own.

No, as long as Amy was in his house, all was well in Dan's world.

~

"Dinner was fabulous, Amy." Dan wiped the corners of his mouth with the linen napkin and heaved a contented sigh. "That dessert—"

"It was good, wasn't it, Daddy?" Emma's blue eyes sparkled the way they always did when her father was in the room.

"It certainly was, princess." Dan's fond smile lingered on his daughter. "Amy is a great cook." Amy pushed back her chair and rose, unable to stop the warm flush of pleasure at the compliment. There was nothing she enjoyed more than trying new recipes. She hadn't been sure how Emma and Dan would react to the citrus-glazed salmon, but she'd been fairly certain they'd love the sour cream peach pie with homemade ice cream.

"Can I get either of you anything else before I clear the table?" Amy's gaze shifted from Dan to Emma.

"No, thank you," Emma said.

Amy shot the little girl a smile of approval. She'd been working with Emma the last couple of months on her manners and it was obviously paying off.

"How about you?" Amy's gaze settled on Dan. She'd lived in his house for over three years and sometimes felt she knew him better than he knew himself. Like now, she couldn't help but notice the lines of fatigue edging his eyes. Lately he'd been working too hard...and socializing too much.

Last Friday night, she'd lain awake until 1:00 a.m. waiting for him to come home before she'd finally fallen asleep. She wasn't sure what time he'd come in but the next morning he'd been at the table at eight, ready to take Emma to the zoo as promised. Saturday night he'd stayed in. They'd all gone to the park and had a picnic, then came home and played board games on the porch until it was time to go to bed.

Being home on a Saturday night had been just one of the signs that another of Dan's relationships had come to an end. It hadn't surprised her. Melinda had been calling a lot and trying to cozy up to Emma. Amy could have told her such behavior was the kiss of death. Once a woman was too eager, Dan lost interest. That's why Amy had kept a tight lid on her burgeoning desire for him. As far as he knew, she didn't feel anything more for him than simple friendship. She was his housekeeper, his daughter's caregiver and his friend.

Occasionally he'd confide in her, knowing what he said wouldn't go any further. She savored those times and the closeness she...

"Earth to Amy." Dan's voice broke through her reverie.

She looked up with a start to find Dan and Emma staring at her.

Emma giggled. "You were spacing out."

Amy blinked and warmth crept up her neck. "What were you thinking about?" Dan asked, a curious glint in his eye. "You had the most interesting smile on your face."

I was thinking about you.

The words rose unbidden to her tongue and when Emma giggled again, for a second Amy feared she'd said them aloud. She searched for a plausible explanation. "I was thinking about Steven."

"Steven?" Dan frowned. "Who's that?"

"He's her boyfriend," Emma said. "Amy and Steven sittin' in a tree, K-I-S-S-I-N-G. First comes love—"

"You were kissing a man?" The shocked look on Dan's face would have been funny at any other time. "In front of Emma?"

"I wasn't, I didn't," Amy said quickly, embarrassed warmth coloring her cheeks. She shifted her gaze to Emma. "Steven is my friend, not my boyfriend."

"You talked to him for a long time on the phone today," Emma said. "You were smiling when you hung up."

"He's my *friend*," Amy repeated- She glanced at Dan. "I've told you about him. He's the guy from my cooking club. We were exchanging lasagna recipes."

Dan's dimple flashed. "Lasagna recipes?"

"That's right." Amy lifted a brow. "You find that amusing?"

"Not at all," Dan said smoothly. "I think it's nice that you two have so much in common."

Amy pulled her brows together, not sure if he was being serious or insulting.

"We both like to cook," she said finally.

Dan's finger traced the raised pattern on the lace tablecloth and when he spoke his tone was decidedly offhand. "You two have been going out for what— a couple of months now?"

"Something like that," Amy said. She still didn't think of Steven as a boyfriend since, until recently, most of the "dates" had revolved around cooking group events.

Something flickered in the back of Dan's eyes but he remained silent.

Unexpectedly Emma lifted her gaze to Amy. "Do you love him like my daddy loved my mommy?"

The girl's question took Amy by surprise and she answered honestly. "No, I don't."

"Do you think you *could* love him?" Dan asked.

"I don't know," Amy said when she realized Dan expected an answer. "I guess anything is possible."

Dan tucked Emma into bed and reveled at this perfect child he and Tess had created. He loved her with an intensity that took his breath away and his heart ached at the thought of all the pain she'd had to endure in her short life. All because of his selfish desire to give her a brother or sister.

"Good night, princess." He brushed a kiss across her cheek. She was his priority and nothing mattered more to him than ensuring her happiness. "I love you."

"I love you, too, Daddy."

"Amy will be up in a minute to say good-night." His stomach tightened into a knot. Usually he and Amy tucked Emma in together. Tonight, *Steven* had called and Amy had said to go on without her.

A tear trailed down Emma's cheek and her brows pulled together. With her big blue eyes and honey- blond hair, she looked more and more like her mother every day.

Dan's heart tightened. "What's the matter, sweetie?"

The little girl's bottom lip trembled and a few more tears fell. Though Dan wanted to make better whatever was bothering her, he forced himself to wait. He'd learned you couldn't rush Emma. When she was ready, she'd tell him what was bothering her. *Then* he'd make it all better.

"Is Amy going to marry Steven?"

The words hit Dan like a punch to the chest. He realized he couldn't imagine his life without Amy in it. He'd fought a surge of jealousy each time she went out with Steven by reassuring himself they were only friends. Somehow, he managed to keep a smile on his lips. "She said he was just her friend. Remember?"

"Sometimes friends get married." Emma pushed herself up to her elbows. "When Grandma Ann married Grandpa Hal she said he was her good friend."

Dan's mother had been widowed for many years when she and her old friend Hal had decided to tie the knot. Theirs wasn't the romantic love she and his father had shared but they were content together. Even if Dan could explain it adequately, he wasn't sure a six-year-old could understand.

"Daddy." Emma's voice trembled. "Amy's not going to marry him and leave us, is she?"

Dan's jaw clenched at the thought of his daughter enduring one more loss. He knew it wasn't just Emma who'd suffer. If Amy left it would leave a hole in both their hearts.

"She's not going to leave." He pulled Emma close and planted a kiss against her hair. "Not if I have anything to say about it."

The resolve in Dan's heart resounded in his voice. He didn't care what the cost. He'd do whatever it took to keep Amy with him...and Emma happy.

CHAPTER THREE

After leaving Emma, Dan took the back stairs to the kitchen. He rummaged through the refrigerator for several minutes before he realized he wasn't hungry or thirsty.

Grabbing his phone, Dan headed to the porch to check the news. Perhaps reading about people with real troubles would help him forget his own.

Amy wasn't going to leave, he told himself. He paid her well and she loved taking care of Emma. As far as that guy Steven was concerned, if he was truly interested in Amy he wouldn't be talking about *recipes* with her.

Reassured by his logic, Dan opened the paper and turned to the financial section. He'd barely started reading when he heard footsteps.

Amy pushed the screen door open with her shoulder. "Thought you might like a snack."

Dan jumped to his feet and took the tray from her. The faint scent of lilacs teased his nostrils. It was an old-fashioned scent but one that suited her. He glanced down.

A thin slice of lemon topped each glass of lemonade and the

assorted cookies perfectly arranged on the decorative plate looked like they could have come from a gourmet bakery.

"These look fabulous," he said.

Amy blushed a becoming shade of pink and took a seat in a wicker chair.

Dan placed the tray on the tiny table in between the two chairs, handed her a glass and took the other for himself.

Though he still wasn't particularly thirsty, she'd gone to a lot of work and Dan wasn't about to disappoint her. He lifted a glass to his lips and took a long sip. "Perfect."

Satisfaction filled Amy's gaze. "It's always better when the lemons are freshly squeezed."

"You squeezed these?"

She laughed—a pleasant laugh that reminded Dan of the tinkle of bells. "With my own two hands." Dan didn't need to ask if she'd made the cookies. They were too perfect *not* to be hers.

"Snickerdoodle." He filched one from the center of the plate. "My favorite."

"I think I knew that," Amy said with a teasing smile. Dan returned her smile and decided he'd been foolish to worry. Amy was happy with him and Emma. She wasn't going anywhere.

She glanced at the news pulled up on his phone. "Anything interesting?"

"Stock market is up today." They drank lemonade, ate cookies and read in comfortable silence. Dan never felt pressured to make small talk with Amy. If there was something to discuss, it was brought up. Otherwise, it was okay to just relax.

Dan wasn't sure when he first became aware that Amy was doing more than just reading her tablet. Maybe it was when he noticed her making quick marks on the screen with the stylus.

What was she doing?

He could ask but he already felt like he'd gone over the line at dinner and didn't want to overstep again. Amy was a private person and Dan had always subscribed to the notion that if she wanted him to know something, she'd tell him.

"Jake and I stopped for a drink after work." Dan hoped if he started talking, so would she. "You'll never guess who I saw."

Amy cocked her head. "Who?"

"Bree Northcott." Dan wasn't sure why he'd brought the woman up, other than she'd been one of the few women he'd dated Amy had seemed to genuinely like. "She was the blonde who—"

"I remember Bree." A warm look filled Amy's eyes. "And Kelly cat and Todd."

Dan paused. "Who?"

Amy giggled. "Her cats. A Scottish Fold and an Abyssinian."

The words meant nothing to him. He only remembered one was furry and the other short-haired.

"Those Scottish Folds are so beautiful." An almost dreamy lilt filled Amy's voice and her lips curved upward. "So difficult to find."

"I don't know anything about cats."

Amy's smile vanished. "That's because you don't like them."

"You're right," Dan admitted. When he'd been small, his neighbor's Siamese had gone ballistic when he'd tried to pick it up. Ever since that day, Dan had given all felines a wide berth. "I don't like them. I'd certainly never want one, let alone two, in my house. Thankfully Tess and I agreed on that."

Amy's expression didn't waver but her gaze shifted back to the screen.

He had the feeling he'd missed something. A sudden thought struck him.

"Emma hasn't mentioned wanting a kitten, has she?" Though Dan would give his daughter the sun and moon if he could, he drew the line at a cat.

"Not to me." Amy's gaze remained fixed on the tablet.

Dan heaved a sigh of relief. "Good."

"She'd never ask because she knows how you feel about them," Amy added.

Though she'd made the comment matter-of- factly, Dan could have sworn he heard an underlying hint of reproach. He frowned. "Are you saying Emma is afraid to talk to me?"

"Not afraid," Amy said. "She—"

A loud boom of thunder split-the air and Amy jumped. The tablet slid from her lap and the napkins on the tray flew off in a gust of wind.

Dan met Amy's gaze and the concern in her eyes mirrored his own. "Emma."

His daughter was deathly afraid of storms and the thunder had been loud enough to wake the dead, let alone a light sleeper.

"You go." Amy made a shooing motion. "I'll stay and pick up."

The wind began to blow in earnest, ruffling her hair and threatening to topple the empty lemonade glasses.

Dan shook his head. "She'll want you, not me."

Though it pained him to say so, it was the truth. During thunderstorms, it was always Amy who Emma clung to, not him.

Amy nodded and touched his arm. "Thanks."

Another loud clap of thunder rent the air.

Amy hurried off before he could ask why she was thanking him. After the door slammed shut, a few drops of rain plopped on the sidewalk and Dan didn't have time to think. He'd lived in the Midwest long enough to know he needed to hurry. After scooping up her tablet and sliding the phone into his pocket, Dan grabbed the plate of cookies and empty glasses and headed inside.

He'd barely made it through the door when the rain began in earnest, the wind spraying droplets of water across the floor of the porch.

By the time Dan reached the kitchen, sheets of rain pelted the windows. He placed the cookies and glasses on the counter and set her tablet down.

Though Dan told himself it was none of his business, he found his gaze drawn to the circled items.

An icy chill traveled up his spine. Real estate in the suburbs? The price range seemed a little out of her league, but it might be manageable, depending on the size of the down payment or if there were two incomes.

Steven.

Had she lied when she'd said the two of them were just friends? In his heart he didn't think so. Still, she'd mentioned more than once how much she longed for a house of her own.

His gaze remained fixed on the tablet. Dan couldn't imagine this home without Amy. If she left, Emma would be devastated. He, well, he would miss her.

Amy wouldn't leave, he reminded himself, because he was committed to doing whatever it took to make her stay. He just had to find out what it would take to keep Amy in his home and in his life.

Amy leaned back in the rocker and sighed with contentment. Though she knew many would say Emma was too big or too old to be rocked, Amy enjoyed being close to the little girl.

Emma had run into her arms when she'd entered the bedroom. Amy had learned long ago she couldn't talk Emma out of her fear; what reassured and calmed her most was to be held. So, she'd taken a seat in the wooden rocker and Emma had crawled onto her lap. For a long moment Amy had just held her close. Once Emma's tears had stopped, Amy had started to sing. Her voice hadn't been good enough to make Swing Choir in high school but Emma didn't complain. These songs from past and present Broadway musicals were Emma's lullabies.

Now Emma slept, her cheeks still showing remnants of the tears that had flowed so freely only minutes before. Amy stroked the little girl's hair and wondered if Tess had ever rocked Emma to sleep and marveled at this perfect child she'd created. Amy liked to think so. She let her mind drift back to the time she'd first met Tess.

She remembered her vividly—the wispy blond hair, the pretty elfin features and the immense blue eyes. Tess had been a petite dynamo who could charm the socks off a complete stranger and bring her handsome husband to his knees with a single smile.

Tess had been three months from delivering her second baby when Amy had first come to live in the Major household. Even pregnant Tess had been cute and trendy, a fashionista on the cutting edge of the latest styles.

Emma had been almost three, a shy, sensitive child who reminded Amy more of herself than of her gregarious parents. Shortly after Amy had arrived Tess had confided that she found it hard to understand how a child of hers could have so many fears.

Perhaps because she'd been plagued with those same insecurities, Amy had felt a kinship with Emma. They'd bonded immediately, which was good considering Tess hadn't been around much.

Tess had been launching a new line and all her time and attention had been focused on work. When Amy had casually asked Dan if Tess planned to keep up this pace after the baby was born, he'd just laughed and said Tess wasn't happy unless she was going ninety miles an hour.

Amy wasn't sure if Dan was kidding or not. Surely Tess planned to slow down and spend some time with Emma once the baby was born. In the end, Tess never got that chance. The placenta had unexpectedly separated from the uterine wall and, despite a valiant effort by emergency personnel, she and the baby had died.

Even after three years the memory of that night still made Amy's heart ache. It had been such a horrible time in all their lives...

"Is everything okay?" Dan's voice sounded from the doorway.

Ducking her head, Amy shoved the memories aside. Though she knew Tess was never far from Dan's thoughts, he never talked about that period and she never brought it up.

She leaned her cheek against the top of Emma's head and gained her composure. "Emma was frightened, but she calmed right down."

Amy sensed, rather than saw, Dan move across into the room. He squatted by the rocker and touched her arm. The feel of his hand against her skin took her by surprise and reminded her of her earlier daydream. Her heart flip-flopped in her chest.

"I was asking about you," he said.

"Me?" Her voice came out as a high-pitched squeak and Amy nearly groaned aloud wondering what had happened to her normally unflappable composure.

"You haven't been yourself lately," he said softly. "Is there anything you want to tell me?"

Amy met his gaze and her breath caught. Something flickered in his eyes and she wondered if he felt the electricity, too. When she looked again, only simple concern reflected back at her.

"I'm just fine." Amy forced a bright smile. "Everything is great."

"Is there anything you want?" Once again, his gaze searched hers. "Anything at all?"

Dear God, it was like her fantasy had come to life. The spicy scent of his cologne wafted about her and something quivered deep in Amy's belly. Perspiration dotted her brow.

His gaze locked with hers and Amy could feel herself being pulled into the blue depths.

"What is it you want, Amy?" he asked again. "Tell me and I'll give it to you."

Amy searched his face, looking for what she wasn't sure.

I want you. The words hovered on the edges of her lips. *Take me in your arms and kiss me.*

As much as she longed to say the words, Amy had learned the hard way what happens when you're needy and demanding.

"It doesn't take much to make me happy," Amy said finally, not really answering his question.

His brows drew together and he appeared to consider her words. After a moment he rose to his feet.

"Let me take her." He held out his arms. "The storm has passed. She should sleep all night now."

With well-practiced ease, Dan scooped Emma into his arms and lifted her to his chest.

Amy's breath caught at the look of love on his face. She'd been scarcely older than Emma when her beloved father had been killed in a car accident. She'd never experienced such unconditional love since.

Emma might not have Tess, but she wasn't alone.

Unexpected tears filled Amy's eyes but thankfully Dan was too busy tucking Emma into bed to notice.

"I'll see you downstairs." Amy rose from the rocker and moved quickly across the glossy hardwood to the door. Dan saw her as a strong, practical woman and she didn't want him to think differently.

Dan brushed a kiss across Emma's cheek and turned to find Amy hurrying toward the door. "Hey, wait for me."

He rose and followed her with his lengthy stride but she didn't slow down. If anything, she increased her pace.

Then, like a scene from a slapstick comedy where someone slips on a banana peel, Amy's feet flew out from under her. A startled cry sprang from her lips.

Dan responded instinctively. With his heart in his throat, he lunged forward and grabbed her from behind. There was no time to think. No time to consider where to place his hands.

Amy wore a bra, but the moment his hand gripped the soft mound of flesh, the contact might as well have been skin-to-skin.

She gasped and turned, her cheeks two bright spots of pink. He immediately dropped his arms to his sides and took a step back. Heat rose up his neck.

While Amy's face gave nothing away, her hand trembled as she carefully straightened her shirt.

Guilt coursed through Dan. He captured her gaze, willing her to see by the look in his eyes that he was sincerely sorry. "Amy, I—"

"Daddy?" Emma's sleepy voice sounded from across the room.

Dan whirled. He'd barely taken a step when Emma snuggled into her pillow and her eyelids drifted shut.

"Love you, Daddy. Love you, Amy."

"Love you, princess," Dan called softly, but the girl was already asleep.

Dan took a deep breath and turned back to Amy.

"Thanks for catching me," she said, not giving him a chance to continue his apology. "I'm usually not so clumsy."

"I'm usually not so rough." Dan shoved his hands into his pockets. "I didn't even realize where I was—"

"I was thinking of making some hot cocoa." Amy offered him a bright smile.

Hot cocoa? It was seventy degrees outside.

The desperation in her smile told him all he needed to know. She preferred to pretend nothing had happened.

Dan returned her smile, relieved they wouldn't have to have an awkward discussion.

Amy lifted her gaze, her tongue nervously moistening her lips, her eyes wide and very green. "Want some?"

It was a simple question but Dan's body put its own spin on the words. Heat flowed through his veins like molten lava and he suddenly felt like a hormone-ravaged teenager. The intense feelings took him by surprise. Feeling crazy was one thing. Acting crazy something else entirely.

This was Amy, after all.

"Dan?" she prompted, her voice sounding oddly breathless. "Hot cocoa?"

He shook his head. "I'm not in the mood."

Not for hot cocoa, anyway.

Amy met his gaze and her cheeks darkened to a deep rose. For a second he had the sinking feeling she could read his thoughts.

"Suit yourself." She waved an airy hand. "I'll be in the kitchen if you change your mind."

After she left, Dan checked Emma one last time before heading for the stairs. This morning, he hadn't a care in the world. Now, he was lusting after his daughter's nanny and he had nothing but worries.

As he approached the kitchen, he could hear Amy humming. The Broadway show tune sung a trifle off-key told him more than words that he hadn't completely screwed up. At least not yet.

The last remnants of tension eased from his shoulders and Dan decided that maybe he was in the mood for that cup of hot cocoa after all.

CHAPTER FOUR

I understand you're upset about your neighbor dying in that car accident." Dan spoke in a soothing tone, even as he tightened his fingers around the phone. He'd been sympathetic for the first twenty minutes of his mother-in-law's call, but his patience was wearing thin. For the last half hour she'd talked nonstop about George, her neighbor, and how he wouldn't have died if he'd heeded her advice and not ridden his bike after dark.

It didn't help that Dan had had a particularly crummy weekend. Amy had gone out with Steven on Friday night and Emma had been cranky.

Today he'd thought they'd all go biking down by the lake after breakfast and maybe catch some lunch at Navy Pier, but once again Amy had plans with Steven. Dan couldn't help but wonder if she was deliberately avoiding him...

"—Emma's welfare."

Dan realized with a start that while his thoughts had been wandering, Gwen had continued to ramble.

"What did you say about Emma?" He relaxed his hold on the phone. There was nothing he liked better than talking about Emma with her doting grandparents. In fact, he'd tried to steer the conversation around to Emma several times in the last thirty minutes but Gwen had been too focused on her neighbor.

"I said you need to make sure that your will names us as Emma's guardians if anything happens to you."

Dan forced a halfhearted laugh. "Nothing is going to happen to me."

"We all think that," Gwen said. "My neighbor George didn't plan to die and neither did my daughter."

Though Gwen had never come right out and said it, Dan knew she blamed him for Tess's death. Tess wouldn't have gotten pregnant a second time if he hadn't been so adamant about wanting another child.

"I've already made provisions for Emma In that unlikely event."

A moment of stunned silence filled the phone line.

"I'm surprised your mother would agree." Gwen's tone pitched high. "What with having a new husband and all."

"My mother didn't think she'd have the stamina for a young child." Dan had been disappointed but he appreciated his mom's candor. "A friend here in Chicago has agreed to raise Emma if something happens to me."

After his mother said no, Dan had approached Amy who'd been touched by the request.

"A friend?" Gwen's voice rose. "Who is this person? Have I met him?"

Dan hesitated. Gwen had been wealthy her entire life. In her mind a nanny was a servant and as such would never be considered an appropriate guardian for her only grandchild.

"Emma belongs with family," Gwen continued when Dan didn't respond. It wasn't so much what she said as how she said it that reminded him of Tess. Spunky Tess, who used to lift her chin and show him her stubborn face when they disagreed.

Some of his irritation dissolved in the remembrance. Gwen and Phil had loved their daughter and they loved Emma. Unfortunately, they could be harsh and unyielding in their views. Dan had no doubt, given time and opportunity, they'd end up crushing Emma's gentle spirit.

Even now, he had to monitor their interactions with her. They compared Emma to Tess at every opportunity and Emma always came up lacking.

"My mind is made up." Dan kept his tone equitable. "I'm not going to change it."

"Well, if anything happens, this friend of yours will have a fight on his hands." His mother-in-law's voice turned frosty. "We will not let our granddaughter be taken from us. I happen to know that family is always given extra weight in custody issues."

Dan's knuckles turned white at her obvious disregard for his wishes.

C'mon, Dan. I know she can be difficult, but be nice to them. Please. For me.

The memory of Tess's familiar plea stopped his sharp retort. Instead Dan forced a conciliatory tone.

"Gwen, it's been great talking to you but I need to go." He ignored her murmur of protest. "Be sure and tell Phil hello."

Dan said good-bye quickly and ended the call before she could get another word out. Though he had a thousand and one things to do, he didn't move a muscle. He sat staring at the phone, cursing his mother-in-law's high-handedness and wondering what in the world he was going to do now.

Dan sat at the kitchen table. After making a few swipes on his phone, he tried to focus on the latest stock market reports but his gaze kept straying to Amy. She'd returned from her afternoon with Steven in a lighthearted mood. Her skin was rosy from the sun and her green eyes sparkled like emeralds. She looked, he thought, uncommonly pretty today.

When she leaned over to put the casserole in the oven, he found himself staring at her smooth thighs and the rounded curves of her breasts.

~

Dan inhaled a deep, steady breath. This had to stop. He really hated that his gaze lingered on those long, supple legs. He didn't like noticing the way her shirt clung to every curve or just how nice those curves were.

This was all Jake's fault, he thought irritably. If he hadn't mentioned Amy dating, Dan wouldn't have looked at her in that way at all. For three years she'd been his daughter's nanny. Now, all of a sudden, he'd realized she was a woman, too.

Oblivious to the turmoil her shapeliness was causing, Amy closed the lower oven door and turned. "Have I told you how much I love this double oven?"

Her cotton top accentuated her full, generous breasts, and for a fleeting moment Dan found himself wondering what she'd look like naked. His mouth went dry and it took everything he had to return her smile and concentrate on the question. "Only about a million times."

She laughed. "I think you're exaggerating just a bit."

The sound of her laughter made him smile. Maybe he was exaggerating, but Dan had no doubt the reason she'd been so content in his household had a lot to do with the kitchen. Last year he'd had the entire area redone and Amy had supervised the construction. Since she used it the most, it had only made sense she should have input into the final product.

She'd been so thrilled with the results that when the last contractor had walked out the door, in a moment of pure joy she'd thrown her arms around Dan's neck and given him a hug. He hadn't given it a second thought. Afterward she'd been embarrassed, but he'd understood. She'd just been given her dream kitchen on a silver platter.

But it wasn't really her kitchen.

Was that why Amy continued to date Steven? Amy was practical. The Lasagna Man might not make her heart beat faster—not yet anyway—but he could give her companionship and a permanent home of her own.

So could I...

The thought surprised him. He shoved it aside but it immediately boomeranged back. This time he considered the idea. He and Amy shared many common interests and most importantly, they both loved Emma. In a way, he and Amy hooking up made its own kind of sense.

Dan glanced at his watch and headed to the back porch. When Amy got home, he'd be waiting.

Amy shifted her gaze out the window of Steven Mitchell's lakeshore condo. The lights of Chicago blinked back at her. All evening she'd found herself mesmerized by the view.

Her lips curved up in a smile. It had been a wonderful evening, thanks to her very gracious host. She turned back to tell him that but before the words could leave her lips, Steven reached across his dining room table and took her hand.

She wasn't surprised he'd gotten caught up in the mood. Though that's not how it had been intended, the evening had taken a decidedly romantic turn. Crystal glittered in the candlelight and classical music in the background added to the ambience.

"Dinner was fabulous." In the dim light, Steven's eyes looked more black than gray. "You really outdid yourself."

Amy resisted the urge to gently remove her hand from his grasp. It wasn't that she minded holding hands with Steven, she just didn't want him to get the wrong idea. After all, she'd meant it when she'd told Dan that she and Steven were merely cooking buddies. Though it was beginning to look like Steven might want more...

"Simply fabulous." Steven breathed the words, his gaze riveted to her.

Amy forced herself to chew and swallow. She wasn't sure why Steven was laying it on so thick but she couldn't help but be flattered. Still she forced a nonchalant air as if having a handsome man flirt with her was an everyday occurrence.

"Beef tenderloin can be so boring." Amy lifted the wineglass to her mouth with her free hand. "The secret is the parsley sauce with cornichons and capers."

"You have just the right touch." Steven's thumb caressed her palm and Amy almost inhaled her Merlot.

What was happening? The stars definitely had to be in some kind of funky alignment. First, she'd found herself practically salivating over Dan and now Steven—who'd always respected the boundaries she'd set—seemed determined to push into new territory tonight.

Amy had the feeling she was partially to blame. Two weeks ago, when Steven had taken her to a fancy French restaurant, she'd happened to mention how tired she was of cooking the same boring meals that were Dan and Emma's favorites. She longed to cut loose and try some fun, fancy recipes for a change.

Steven had immediately jumped on the idea. He'd suggested that every week they take turns making each other a meal of their own choosing. Last week Steven had treated her to a fabulous evening of Indian cuisine.

Tonight had been her turn to shine. When she'd agreed to the plan, she hadn't considered *where* she would prepare a meal when it was *her* turn. After all, she could hardly use Dan's kitchen to entertain Steven.

When she'd said as much to Steven, he'd merely smiled and offered her the use of his place. Unfortunately the only night this week that worked for him was Sunday, a day usually reserved for Dan and Emma. But Steven was going out of town on business for two weeks and he'd insisted he couldn't wait that long to see what treat she had in store for him.

"Amy." Steven's husky, deep voice broke through her reverie. "Have I told you how beautiful you look this evening?"

Amy lifted her eyes to find his gaze focused on the cleavage displayed by the silky black cocktail dress. Her face heated beneath his admiring gaze and she shifted uncomfortably in her chair. Dressing up for the evening had been Steven's idea. She'd been a bit hesitant, but had decided to go along with the suggestion.

It certainly had helped set the elegant, romantic mood. Of course, the fact that Steven's condo overlooked the lakefront didn't hurt, either. The first time he'd brought her up here, she'd been stunned. In class, dressed in blue jeans, he'd seemed like just another food devotee. Sure, she'd known he was an attorney, she just hadn't realized he was so wealthy. Or so...attractive.

The tuxedo he wore emphasized his lean, muscular build. Like Dan, his hair was dark and cut short, but instead of being blue, Steven's eyes were a piercing gray. She could see why he was so successful in the courtroom. Those eyes missed little.

"I'm flattered," she said.

"You don't believe my compliment." His brows pulled together in puzzlement. "Why is that?"

This time Amy gave in to the urge and slipped her hand from his, nervously brushing back a stray strand of hair from her face.

She wondered if he'd be as impressed if he knew that the black cocktail dress she wore had been purchased at a consignment boutique. Even she had to admit the cut flattered her full, firm breasts while minimizing her curvy hips. She'd pulled her hair back in a loose, French knot and taken extra care with her makeup. At the last minute she'd impulsively added the pair of diamond earrings Dan and Emma had given her last Christmas.

"Amy."

She blinked, realizing his question hadn't been simply rhetorical.

"Beautiful?" Amy forced a laugh. "C'mon, Steven. Even you have to admit I fall in the nice-looking but definitely-not-beautiful range."

She made the observation without the slightest hint of guile. She wasn't fishing for compliments. She was, quite simply, stating the facts.

Still, she half expected Steven to argue. Instead he laughed, the tiny lines around his eyes crinkling. "No wonder I like you so much."

There it was again, a shift into the personal realm. The smoldering look in his eyes told her if she didn't shut it down now, things could get uncomfortable.

"Did I tell you Chez Gladines at Navy Pier has contracted with me to provide French pastries on a trial basis?" Amy couldn't keep the note of pride from her voice. "Apparently their chef had been a real prima donna and an expensive one to boot. When she up and quit on them, they decided to give me a chance."

While the restaurant manager hadn't given Amy a long-term commitment, at least she had a foot in the door.

"Congratulations." A smile split Steven's face. "I wish I'd known earlier, I'd have taken you out to celebrate."

Amy had waited to mention the news for that specific reason. She didn't want to give him the chance to act like a boyfriend. He was doing enough of that already. Last time they'd eaten out, he'd refused to let her pay her share. If he *were* her boyfriend, she'd be all about letting him treat her. But they were simply good friends and that's how she wanted to keep it

She let her gaze linger on his handsome face. Steven was a great guy with all the qualities she was looking for in a man. Why couldn't she like him as more than a friend? Why couldn't she love him? What was holding her back?

Amy smiled and held out her glass for more wine.

After filling her glass, Steven leaned back in his chair and shot her a speculative gaze. "What did King Dan have to say?"

Amy rolled her eyes. Steven had never met Dan but he'd taken in a few of her comments and decided he didn't like the guy. Like when she'd mentioned once in passing how much Dan liked to be waited on, she'd never expected Steven to take the funny, little incident and make a big deal out of it.

"Was he happy for you?" Steven pressed.

Amy shrugged and took a sip of wine. "I haven't mentioned it to him yet."

"Why not?" Steven lifted a sardonic brow. "Too busy making his coffee?"

"Making the coffee pays the bills." Amy kept her tone deliberately light and offhand, refusing to get sucked into rehashing something that had already been discussed. Still, it seemed no matter how many times she tried to tell Steven taking care of Dan and Emma was her job, he always tried to push her to think of herself, too.

"I know why you haven't told him. You're afr—"

"The opportunity hasn't come up." Amy spoke slowly and distinctly so there would be no misunderstanding. "When I *do* tell him—and I plan to tell him—I know he'll be happy for me."

"Don't kid yourself." Genuine concern filled Steven's gaze. "If he had it his way, you'd never leave. Never go on to bigger and better things. You deserve your own dreams, too, Amy."

The unexpected vehemence in Steven's tone took her by surprise. She just smiled because she knew he really meant well. He was wrong about Dan...and about her.

CHAPTER FIVE

Amy shut off the car's ignition and leaned back against the seat, too tired to get out. The clock on the dashboard read eleven forty-five and exhaustion oozed from every pore. Her normal bedtime was ten- thirty and when she'd started to yawn while discussing the merits of using liqueurs, she'd known it was time to head home.

As she started toward the door, Steven had pulled her close and kissed her. Then he'd asked if she'd consider spending the night. The crazy thing was, for a second, she'd been tempted. It had been so long...

In the end she'd said no, frightened by the serious look in his eyes and her own ambivalent feelings. Besides, there was only one man she wanted in that way and he was waiting for her at home.

The garage door slid smoothly downward and, heaving a resigned sigh, Amy stepped out of the car and headed for the side door. Unlike Steven's condo with its underground parking, Dan's house had been built in the early 1900s when detached carriage houses were de rigueur.

Amy didn't mind the short walk to the house. The temperature had dropped slightly and the autumn coolness was a welcome break from the warmth of the car. She could feel herself begin to wake up.

How she loved the lush yard with its large trees and beautiful arbors and the way the fragrant smell of flowers mixed with the scent of freshly-cut grass. During the day squirrels chattered a mile a minute and birds chirped happily. Now all was quiet. She stopped just short of the house and inhaled, taking in the beauty around her.

Amy vowed that when she bought a house it would have a nice yard. She remembered all too well the tiny apartment she'd shared with her aunt after her mother had dropped her off and never came back. She'd had to play outside on the concrete...

Shoving the memory aside, she decided it was too nice a night to ruin with thoughts of the past. She should go straight to bed but the idea of sitting for a few minutes in one of the large Adirondack chairs on the back screened-in porch pulled at her.

It would be so peaceful, so—

"How was your evening?"

The familiar deep voice stopped her cold. Dan sat in one of the chairs on the porch. She could count on one hand the number of times he'd stayed up past ten-thirty on a work night. Concern rippled up her spine. She moved forward quickly, her heart picking up speed with each step. "Where's Emma? Is everything okay?"

"She's fine." Dan rose and held the porch door open. "Went to bed for me without any problem." Amy exhaled the breath she'd been holding. "So nothing is wrong?"

"Why would you think something is wrong?"

"You're up," Amy said. "You're always in bed by now."

"You're dressed up." His gaze traveled the length of her body. Amy could hear the surprise in his tone and though she wasn't a bit cold, she shivered.

He'd known she was going out with Steven. He'd been

upstairs when she'd left and had obviously assumed this had been a jeans and T-shirt evening.

"I made dinner for Steven at his place."

"He made you cook?" Dan's brows pulled together and she could hear the censure in his tone. "When you were dressed like that?"

Amy heaved an exasperated sigh and dropped into a chair. What was it with these men?

"He didn't *make* me do anything." Amy kicked off her heels. "We're taking turns cooking each other dinner. Steven likes to dress up. Do things nice. He thinks it adds to the ambience."

Even in the dim light, Amy could see the surprise in Dan's eyes. He opened his mouth, then shut it.

She paused, waiting for him to disagree. After all, that seemed to be the pattern between the two men.

"I agree," Dan said.

"You do?" Amy's voice rose despite her best efforts to control it

"Of course," Dan said, his tone conversational and pleasant

Amy let her shoulders drop and the last of the tension exited her body. Finally, here on this quiet porch, she was back on familiar footing and could relax.

Tonight had not been the evening she'd anticipated. Instead of being the kind, supportive friend, Steven had tried to play the boyfriend card. She'd hated to shut him down but she didn't see that she had much choice. Not when her feelings for Dan were growing stronger. She slanted a sideways glance.

Dan had leaned back in his chair, lacing his fingers behind his head in a relaxed pose. "Does Steven live close?"

"Not far." Though it might not be very Emily Post, Amy brought her foot up and massaged her instep. The stiletto heels might look great but they were a killer. "He lives in one of the condos by the Pier."

The words had barely left her lips when Dan scooted his chair to face hers. "Give me those."

Amy widened her eyes. "Pardon?"

"Your feet," he said. "Those kind of shoes take their toll. I used to give Tess a foot rub all the time. Put them here."

Amy hesitated. While he wasn't suggesting they get naked and jump into bed, what he was suggesting somehow seemed just as intimate. Before she had a chance to respond, he reached down and rested both her feet on top of his muscular thighs.

"Ah—" He began to gently massage her foot from the toes to the ankle and any words of protest died on a sigh.

"You are incredible," she breathed.

The dimple in his left cheek flashed. "Well, thank you, ma'am. I aim to please."

He shifted his focus to the sole of her foot, his fingers moving in circular motions from the base of her toes to the heel, the pressure of the circles steady and even.

Amy closed her eyes and let the waves of pleasure wash over her.

"I don't believe you've ever told me what Steven does for a living."

The question seemed to come from a great distance. Amy's eyelids fluttered as he turned his attention to her toes.

"He's an attorney." Utterly relaxed, Amy leaned her head back against the chair. "I guess he's handled some high-profile cases but I've never heard of them."

Steven had told her more than once about his practice but she must not have been paying very close attention because right now, with Dan's thumbs pressing into the arch of her foot, she couldn't remember any details.

"What's his last name?" Dan asked in a low, soft voice.

"Mitchell." Amy moaned. "Oh, Dan, if I'd have known I was coming home to this, I'd have never stayed out so late."

"That's okay," Dan said in a hypnotic tone. "Next time just remember...there's no place like home."

The sound of the Flight of the Bumblebees sounded near Amy's ear. She brushed at the irritation, her hand connecting with her phone.

It took only a second for her to realize she wasn't on a far-off beach making love to Dan in the sand. She was in her bedroom with her phone emitting the melody she'd set as her alarm. Sitting up, she glanced at the time.

She gasped. The alarm should have gone off an hour ago. She must have set it wrong. The bus would be coming for Emma in twenty minutes and Dan, well, right now he was on his own.

Amy jumped out of bed, but stopped almost instantly, swaying slightly as her hand rose to her pounding head. She'd had only two or three glasses of wine with Steven, but after Dan had finished her foot massage, he'd brought out a bottle of Kendall Jackson and she'd had a couple more glasses.

Unlike her mother, Amy took responsibility for her own actions. She'd pay the price today. She'd never make Emma and Dan suffer.

Ignoring her aching head, she hurried to the bathroom. After splashing cold water on her face, she ran a brush through her hair and pulled the long strands back into a ponytail. A second later her pajamas hit the floor. Grabbing a pair of leggings and a pullover cotton shirt, she dressed as she headed toward the door, snagging a pair of flip-flops on the way. She slid her feet into the shoes and took the stairs down two at a time.

Emma stood in the kitchen on a chair, a box of cereal clasped tightly against her chest. When she caught sight of Amy she smiled and held out the Cheerios.

"Look what I got." Emma thrust the box outward, unbalancing herself.

Her heart in her throat, Amy crossed the room in three quick strides and scooped Emma into her arms. While she knew she should probably scold the child for climbing on the chair, Emma looked so pleased with herself, Amy didn't have the heart.

"Cereal sounds good to me, too." Amy swung the girl to the floor. "How about you get the place mats from the drawer and I'll get the milk and juice."

"Is there room at the table for one more?"

Amy shifted her gaze and her heart skipped a beat. Dan stood in the doorway, dressed casually in khakis and a polo shirt. His appearance answered one of her questions. Obviously today was going to be a work-from-home day.

"There's lots of room." Emma spoke before Amy could answer. "We got a whole box of Cheerios."

"Or I could make French toast? Or eggs and bacon?" Amy asked. Unlike his daughter, Dan had never been a big cereal fan.

"Cheerios sounds good to me."

"Emma, grab an extra place mat for your father." She shifted her gaze to Dan. "Coffee this morning?"

"Extra strong." A teasing glint filled his blue eyes. "Someone kept me up way too late last night." Amy's heart skipped a beat. For a second she let herself believe that Dan was flirting with her. By the time the rich aroma of the breakfast blend filled the air, she'd gotten her emotions—not to mention her foolish thoughts—under control.

"Can I put the bowls on the table?" Emma offered Amy an imploring glance.

"*May* I put the bowls on the table?" Amy corrected, taking the dishes from the cupboard and handing them to Emma along with three spoons. "Yes, you may."

It wasn't long until cereal and juice were on the table along with steaming cups of coffee for her and Dan.

Emma had barely finished spooning the last soggy "o" into her mouth when the school bus honked. Taking one quick sip of orange juice, she pushed back her chair. "May I be excused?"

Amy cast a quick glance over Emma, then smiled and nodded her approval.

"Goodbye, Daddy." Emma gave her father a quick hug. "Bye, Amy."

Another honk sounded and Emma's eyes widened with alarm. She grabbed her backpack and raced through the house. Only a few steps behind, Amy moved to the large parlor window. She watched Emma get on the bus before she returned to the kitchen.

Amy paused in the doorway, surprised to find Dan still sitting at the table, reading the paper. Normally, when Dan worked from home, he headed upstairs to his office once Emma left for school. He looked up briefly when she entered the room, giving her a distracted smile. Amy stuck the cereal bowls and juice glasses in the dishwasher before topping off Dan's coffee and resuming her seat.

Lifting her cup to her lips, she gazed across the table. "I take it you're working from home today."

"Actually, I've decided to take the day off." He raised his gaze from the newspaper. "Want to play hooky with me?"

Amy's shock must have shown on her face because he chuckled. "I've got some time I need to burn before the end of the year. I thought we could go to Long Grove. Check out the antiques. Maybe grab some lunch?"

Amy placed her cup back on the saucer, surprised by the steadiness of her hand. Was she hallucinating or had Dan just asked her out? Her eyes searched his. While she wasn't sure what she'd expected to see, disappointment coursed through her at the simple friendliness reflected there.

"Amy?"

The day Amy had planned flashed before her—a little light housecleaning, replace the zipper on one of Emma's dresses, then try out a new recipe or two. Chez Gladines was closed on Mondays so Amy didn't need to worry about making pastries. There was nothing on her agenda even half as appealing as a day in Long Grove.

She loved the small community with its quaint atmosphere and plethora of antique shops. The few times she'd been there hadn't been nearly long enough.

But to go with Dan?

A thrill of pleasure raced up her spine at the thought of being his date. No, she firmly reminded herself, if she went it'd be as a *friend,* nothing more.

Amy took one last sip of coffee. "Just give me a few minutes to freshen up and do something with this hair."

"You look fine." Dan tilted his head, his gaze slowly surveying her. "Actually, way more than fine."

Her skin warmed beneath the heat of his gaze, but Amy held no illusions. While Tess may have been beautiful enough to hop out of bed and hit the ground running, Amy didn't have that luxury. She shoved back her chair and stood.

"Give me twenty minutes" she called over her shoulder on the way to the stairs.

Dan didn't argue. Instead he cupped his hands around the mug, leaned back in his chair and stared into the dark Columbian brew.

It had been almost midnight before Amy had pulled in the driveway last night. Dinner with someone who was only a cooking "buddy" would never have lasted so long. He'd been wrong to think the Lasagna Man was no threat. He still couldn't believe Steven Mitchell was Amy's "friend." The attorney was well-known in the Chicago area and had a reputation for getting what he wanted, whether that was an acquittal for a client or some young socialite dazzled by his charm.

Dan had been at a couple of large parties where Steven was in attendance. While they'd never been introduced, Dan had noticed the guy never lacked for feminine attention. It would be so easy for a woman to be taken in by a guy like that, a man who knew all the right things to say to get a woman in his bed.

Maybe he already had…

Dan pressed his lips together and his fingers tightened around the coffee cup until his knuckles turned white.

As offensive as it was, Dan let the idea percolate.

Could it be that Amy and Steven were already lovers? While it was *possible,* after a moment of serious contemplation Dan concluded that the relationship between the two hadn't reached that point...yet.

Why would Steven drag his heels? Unless...he'd fallen for Amy. After all, Amy was the kind of woman a man married, not just dated. Maybe, Dan thought, he should be concerned that Steven and Amy hadn't had sex. Still, just the thought of Steven *kissing* Amy set Dan's teeth on edge. Dan couldn't delay any longer. He had to convince Amy that the only place she belonged was here, with him and Emma.

To convince her, he'd have to go the hearts-and- flowers route. It was the only way to reach her. Because, though she'd deny it to her death, Dan knew the truth. Amy Logan was a closet romantic. The books she read always had a happy ending. Her favorite movies were romantic comedies where you walked out of the theater holding hands and feeling good. Such a woman would never be wooed by pure logic.

"I'm ready."

Amy stood in the doorway wearing a skirt, form- fitting sweater and a tentative smile. Her freshly washed hair glistened and she must have applied some makeup because the freckles he liked so much were barely noticeable.

Dan rose and offered her the smile that had been winning him hearts since grade school. When he spoke the words came straight from the heart. "You look absolutely lovely."

A becoming shade of coral colored her cheeks. "I wasn't sure what to wear. I didn't want to dress up too much, but you did mention we'd be going to lunch so I didn't want to be too casual."

His heart warmed. She was chattering the way she always did when she was nervous.

"You look perfect." Dan stepped forward and took her hand. "We're going to have a great day. I guarantee it."

CHAPTER SIX

A trio of tiny bells welcomed Amy and Dan into the small antique shop in Long Grove. Amy paused in the doorway and let memories from her childhood wash over her. Lace curtains at the windows. Shiny hardwood. The smell of cinnamon in the air. All reminiscent of the turn-of-the-century home that had been in her father's family for generations.

After her parents divorced, she'd lived in the old Victorian with him. Those had been the happiest years of her young life.

Impulsively Amy turned. She slipped her hand through Dan's arm and gave it a squeeze.

"Thanks for bringing me here. I adore this place." Her gaze darted around the well-kept cottage which, despite its extensive inventory, somehow managed to give the appearance of being homey rather than cluttered. An old Victrola played a once-popular dance tune in the background. "My aunt Verna would love it, too."

"Is that the aunt in Minnesota?" Dan asked. "The one you lived with after your father died?"

Amy nodded, her gaze lingering on a sterling silver brush and comb set. "She always said if she had a big old house, it'd be filled with antiques."

There had been no rambling two story for her aunt. No house at all. Only a one-bedroom apartment with a fold-out sofa that doubled as a bed. Verna had worked as a secretary in the Mankato school system and her salary had been barely enough for her to live on. When her sister's young daughter had been added to the mix...

"How is Verna doing?" Dan asked in a conversational tone. "I haven't heard you speak of her recently."

"She's good." Amy picked up a Rookwood pottery vase, promptly putting it down when she saw the price. "She retired in May and spent the summer traveling across the country visiting friends. Now she's working on deciding what she wants to do with the rest of her life."

"You think she'll stay in Mankato?"

Amy picked up a Strawberry Shortcake lunch box. She'd had one just like it. Her father had given it to her for her seventh birthday, just weeks before the accident. "Amy?"

She shifted her attention from the lunch box back to the conversation. "I'm sorry. Did you ask me something?"

Dan smiled. "Is your aunt staying in Minnesota?"

"She's not sure." Actually Verna had talked about moving to Chicago so she could be close to Amy. Amy had been checking out real estate in the area and while she'd love to have her aunt in the same town, she wasn't sure it was going to happen. "She took her retirement in a lump sum so it gives her some options." A petite gray-haired woman who reminded Amy of a wren with her bright, shiny eyes and quick movements appeared from behind a large bureau. "May I help you?"

The woman's gaze lowered to Amy's hand and Amy realized she still held the lunch box. She quickly placed it back on the shelf. "We're just browsing." The moment the words left Amy's lips she realized she'd answered for both of them. While Dan hadn't mentioned looking for anything specific he *had* chosen Long Grove with its abundance of antique stores for their excursion.

She turned and lifted her face to him. "Unless you have—"

"Nothing specific in mind." Dan slipped his arm around Amy's shoulders and returned the woman's smile.

"We'll let you know if we have questions." Amy's breath caught in her throat. Thankfully Dan seemed willing to carry the conversation because the minute he'd pulled her close, she'd lost the ability to form a coherent sentence. She told herself the gesture was simply a casual one between friends. The trouble was her body hadn't gotten the message.

As much as Amy longed to give in to the warm tingling that went all the way to her toes, she held tight to her common sense, slipping from the light embrace as if she'd seen something she absolutely couldn't resist. Scanning the aisle, she found what she was looking for in a black and white kitten curled up on a shelf.

Amy shifted her gaze back to the woman. "You have a cat."

The woman beamed like a proud parent "Her name is Oreo. She'll be six months old on Saturday."

"May I hold her?"

The woman nodded. "She spends most days here in the shop, so she's used to strangers."

Amy moved down the aisle, barely aware of the woman and Dan following her. The animal reminded Amy of Mittens, the cat she'd had when she lived with her father. As she drew closer the differences between the two became more apparent. Mittens had been pure black with four white feet while Oreo had white on her chest as well.

"You are so pretty." Her voice rose and she found herself speaking in that high-pitched tone usually reserved for babies and animals.

The kitten stirred and stretched.

Amy bent down and gingerly scooped up the sleeping cat holding it against her chest

Dan's brows pulled together in puzzlement. "I never knew you were such a cat lover."

Amy gently stroked the soft fur. "I had one like this when I was only a little older than Emma."

"Is Emma your daughter?" the woman asked.

Dan smiled, the way he always did when Emma's name was mentioned. "She's six."

"That's such a sweet age." The shopkeeper's gaze turned sharp and assessing. "Do you two have other children?"

It only took a second for Amy to realize that the woman had assumed she and Dan were married. She opened her mouth to clarify but Dan spoke first. "She's our only one," he said.

"You're young," the woman said. "There's plenty of time for more."

Dan gave a noncommittal smile and changed the subject.

The woman stayed with them the entire time they walked around the store, but the minute they exited the shop, there was only one question on Amy's lips. "Why did you let her think we were married? That Emma was *our* child?"

Although it was late September, the sun shone bright overhead. Unfortunately Dan had already slipped on his sunglasses, hiding his eyes.

"What did you want me to say?" he asked, his tone as expressionless as his face. "That you were Emma's *nanny?*"

"I *am* Emma's nanny."

He took off his glasses, his gaze direct, his eyes an intense blue. "You're much more than that."

A warm flush of pleasure stole its way up her neck.

All the way home, Amy found herself pondering the words, sternly admonishing herself every time she was tempted to read too much into them.

By the time they reached the city, she'd decided that what he'd obviously been trying to say was that she was his friend, a part of the family, not just an employee.

They were about ten minutes from home when her cell phone rang. Amy was going to let it go to voice mail but Dan turned down the volume on the radio. Reluctantly she dug the phone out of her purse. Even if Steven hadn't promised to call her before he left town, the ring tone told Amy it was him.

"Hello, beautiful." Steven's deep voice resounded in her ear. "Have you had a good day?"

"I've had a *very* good day." Just thinking about the past few hours brought a smile to her lips. After visiting most of the stores in town, Dan had treated her to lunch at a quaint little cafe. Then they'd topped the day off with a single scoop cone at an old-fashioned ice cream parlor.

"I wish you were coming with me," Steven said. "Boston is beautiful this time of year."

Amy had always wanted to see Boston but she knew if she'd gone that Steven would expect more than just a sightseeing partner.

"I'm sure it is," Amy said. "Tell me again how long you'll be gone?"

"Hopefully not more than two weeks," Steven said. A teasing note sounded in his voice. "Are you going to miss me?"

Amy hesitated. She cast a sideways glance at Dan. His gaze was focused straight ahead on the road. He didn't appear to be listening but...

"Um, hmm." Amy decided to leave it at that.

"Is he there?" Suspicion filled Steven's tone. "Is that why you can't talk?"

Amy forced a casual laugh. "Dan and I are just getting back from Long Grove."

"Listen, Amy," Steven said. "My plane is boarding, so I'll keep this short. You're his employee. That's all you are. That's all you'll ever be. Getting more involved with him would be a mistake."

For a second Amy sat there stunned. Sure, she'd spoken of Dan more often than she probably should but she'd never suggested there was anything between them. Or even that she *wished* there could be more. So why was Steven concerned? Unless she wasn't as good at hiding her emotions as she thought...

Amy could hear the overhead announcing final boarding. "I better let you go."

"A mistake, Amy," Steven said, sounding genuinely concerned. "Don't be fooled. Promise you'll be careful."

"I promise," Amy said, her voice as tight as the fingers gripping the phone. While she found his concern touching, she was horrified at the thought of Dan seeing through her as easily as Steven.

"Good." Though relief flowed through Steven's voice, she could still hear the worry.

Steven didn't give her enough credit.

She knew better than to get involved with Dan.

No matter how much she was tempted.

Dan had never been the type of guy to eavesdrop, but in the small cab of the Land Rover it was impossible *not* to listen.

It didn't take a genius to realize Amy was talking to Steven. As far as Dan was concerned it was a bad sign that the guy had called. Steven had seen her the past three days and yet he still felt the need to touch base today?

Amy slipped the cell phone into her purse. "That was Steven."

"Do you two have plans tonight?" Dan did his best to keep his tone offhand. After all, he couldn't risk appearing disapproving. The last thing he wanted was to push her into Steven's apparently all-too-eager arms.

Amy shook her head. "He's headed to Boston."

"Really?" Dan relaxed against the seat. A thousand miles away was the perfect place for the guy. "What's he going to be doing there?"

"Some case," Amy said. "He didn't go into much detail."

"I'm surprised he didn't ask you to go with him," Dan said, the lightness in his tone at odds with the tightness still gripping his chest.

"He asked," Amy said. "I told him I had obligations here."

Dan didn't know what disturbed him more—that Steven had obviously felt comfortable enough to ask or that Amy had referred to him and Emma as "obligations." "How long will he be gone?"

"Two weeks," Amy said with a sigh. "It might even be longer."

Dear God, she actually sounded like she was going to miss the guy. The relationship must be moving faster than he thought.

Emma's face flashed before him and Dan remembered the promise he'd made her. A promise he fully intended to keep. Though he'd never been impulsive or one to move forward without careful thought, he realized suddenly that his little girl's happiness might depend on his quick action.

Two weeks. More than enough time to make Amy fall in love with me.

It was a crazy thought, but once it flitted through his consciousness, it took hold and wouldn't let go.

Fourteen days.

To become her friend.

To become her lover.

To become her husband.

CHAPTER SEVEN

Amy leaned over Emma, brushed a kiss against the sleeping girl's forehead then tiptoed out of the bedroom.

After dinner the three of them had gone for a long walk. By the time they'd gotten back it had been time for Emma's bath. Amy swore the child was asleep before she'd finished toweling her dry.

"Amy." Dan's voice resonated from the bottom of the stairs. "Could you come down here, please? There's something I'd like to discuss with you."

"Of course." Amy pulled Emma's bedroom door shut, wondering what could be so important that it couldn't wait until morning.

Household concerns were normally discussed after Emma left for school in the morning, never at night. But then, Amy reminded herself, this day had not been "normal" in any sense of the word.

Having workaholic Dan take time off to go shopping had been only the beginning. He'd let the woman in the antique store think they were married, and his reason hadn't made a bit of sense. At dinner he'd been distracted, yet afterward when they'd gone for a walk, he'd been jovial, entertaining her and Emma with funny stories from his boyhood. When they'd stopped at the park, Emma had headed straight for the slide. Amy had started to sit on a nearby bench but Dan had insisted they check out the swings.

She'd laughed. He'd teased. Each time his hands had settled on her waist, Amy's heart had soared higher than the swing.

No. The day had *definitely* not been normal.

Amy hurried down the stairs, eager to find out what could be so important.

Dan smiled when he saw her.

"Come in." He stood outside the parlor and waved her through the doorway.

Although the day had been more like summer, a cheery fire burned brightly in the hearth. The room, which Tess had turned ultramodern shortly before her death had been returned to its original decor two summers ago.

Amy had never been sure if the change had been made because Dan hated the minimal design with the black accents as much as she did or if the room had reminded him too much of Tess. His wife had been as chic and stylish as the room and Amy could only surmise that every time Dan had walked through the door he'd been reminded of what he'd lost.

Dan gestured to a chintz-covered Windsor. "Please sit down."

Amy took a seat, while Dan continued to stand. After a few moments he moved to a spot just in front of the fireplace. He stared into the flames and a flicker of unease inched its way up Amy's spine. Whatever was on his mind was obviously serious. Amy tilted her head. "Is something wrong?"

Dan turned and raked a hand through his hair. He crossed the room and dropped into the chair beside Amy. "I've got something to say and I'm not sure how you're going to respond."

Shifting uneasily in her chair, Amy could feel a chill travel up her spine. This *must* be serious if supremely confident Dan, a man who always knew where he wanted to go and how to get there, was nervous and unsure.

Why? What could he possibly have to say that would cause him such distress?

There was only one thing that made sense. Today had been a gift, one last pleasant day with him and Emma, just like the day her mother had taken her out for ice cream, then dropped her off and never came back.

"You're letting me go." The words slipped past her lips despite her determination to let him speak first.

"No. No. No." Dan leaned forward and took her cold hand, clasping it firmly in his. "That is— No. I'm definitely not letting you go anywhere."

The breath Amy had been holding came out in a whoosh and relief flooded her body. "Then, what...?" "Actually *this* is what I need to discuss with you." Dan cast a pointed glance at their joined hands.

Horrified, Amy realized her fingers now interlocked with his. She tried to pull away but he held on tight, his lips curving upward.

"I'm as bad at this as I thought I'd be." Dan leaned forward, resting his elbows on his knees, his hand still gripping hers. "I like you, Amy. I think...I hope...that you like me, too."

Amy pulled her brows together in a puzzled frown, trying to understand what he was saying and coming up blank.

"Of course I like you," she said finally.

"I'm talking as more than a friend." Dan spoke quickly as if afraid she'd interrupt. "I want us to get to know each other better, see where it might lead." Amy's heart slammed against her ribs. More than a friend? For a second she wondered if she was dreaming. She closed her eyes then opened them. Nothing had changed. She swallowed hard and somehow managed a light tone. "You want us to...date?"

He lifted a brow. "You sound shocked."

Amy forced a laugh and glanced around the room. "Where are the cameras? This has to be some kind of joke."

For a second Dan looked startled, then he grinned. "No wonder I like you so much."

"You don't—" Amy said.

"Not in that way." Dan's smile faded. His gaze turned serious. "Lately there's been this...connection between us. You have to have felt it, too."

Amy could feel the heat rise up her neck. It wasn't really a question and for a second she hoped she wouldn't have to answer. But the watchful look in his eyes told her he expected a response. She paused then slowly nodded, hoping she wouldn't regret the admission.

A look of relief crossed Dan's face. "You agree."

"I agree that sometimes there is this 'energy' between us." Amy carefully chose her words. "I'm not convinced acting on it is in either of our best interests."

"Why do you say that?" Dan asked, his eyes as expressionless as his face.

Amy heaved an exasperated sigh. "How about for starters that I'm your employee?"

"So?"

"So if you get tired of me like you did Bree and Melinda, I'm still around. Taking care of your child. Maintaining your house." She jerked her hand from his. "You have to admit that having an ex-girlfriend living in your home could be awkward."

Amy rose and moved to the fireplace but even the warmth of the flames couldn't drive the chill from her body. She had to be practical. They both had to be practical.

"Anything more than just a simple friendship between us would be a mistake," she continued. "A big mistake."

"I disagree," Dan said, not even taking a second to give the matter some thought. "I'm not going to get tired of having you around. We won't have to worry about—"

"We *do* have to worry." Amy whirled around. "Or at least I do. I like working for you, Dan. I like taking care of Emma. I don't want to do anything to screw that up."

"I don't see how us going out—"

Amy threw up her hands. The guy wasn't stupid. How could he be so clueless? "Because the odds are it's going to be a mistake. Just like your relationship with Bree. Just like Melinda. You—"

"Those women were different." He stood and an odd desperation filled his tone. "You can't compare my relationship with them to you and me."

"Why not?" Amy lifted her chin. "There was probably much more chance of those relationships succeeding than one between us."

"How can you say that?"

"Easy. They're from your social circle." Amy almost added "and they're both beautiful" but decided that made it sound as if she thought he was superficial, which she didn't. "You have similar interests—"

"Hold it right there." Dan's eyes flashed blue fire and he crossed the room in several long strides to stand beside her. "If anyone can get along, it's you and me. Think about it. We've lived together for three years in harmony. How many couples can say that?"

They weren't a couple. She was his employee. Though he didn't seem to want to grasp the subtleties of the differences, they were huge. For one, how did a woman go about dating a man whose laundry she folded?

Besides, Amy knew what would happen if they went out. She'd fall in love with him. She was practically in love with him now or certainly infatuated. It wouldn't be long before she'd get scared, then needy and he'd send her away. Just like her mother had...

"Amy?"

She lifted her gaze and found Dan's eyes filled with a gentleness usually reserved for Emma.

"I know you're scared," he said softly. "Heck, I'm scared, too. I believe there could be something special between us. We'll never know for sure if we don't give it a shot."

His nearness made it difficult to think, to be objective. She told herself she needed space, time to consider what he was suggesting. But when he offered her a crooked smile, the raw hunger she'd been keeping in check surged. When she raised her hands, instead of increasing the distance between them, she pulled him to her and closed her mouth over his. She quickly discovered that reality easily outshone even the most wonderful of daydreams.

Dan changed the angle of the kiss and deepened it, shifting one hand to cup the back of her head, holding her still for the hot, sweet hunger of his mouth on hers.

Amy welcomed the moist heat and the penetrating slide of his tongue and met it with her own. He stroked long and slow, hot and deep, and she kissed him back the same way, eagerly and instinctively.

A shivering...sliding feeling ran down her spine and when he pulled her so tight she could feel his arousal against her belly, the world exploded in a blistering wave of heat and passion.

He scattered kisses along her jawline, down her neck and then...lower still.

Her breasts strained against the bodice of her dress and when his tongue dipped into her cleavage, she heard herself groan, a low sound of want and need that astonished her with its intensity. Dazed and breathing hard, Amy pulled back.

There was shock in Dan's eyes. "Amy, I..."

"It's late," she said, her breath coming in ragged puffs. "Let's talk tomorrow."

Without giving him the chance to change her mind, Amy

headed for the hall. She moved quickly, not stopping until she'd reached her room and locked the door behind her.

Utterly confused, Amy sank down on the bed. Her fingers rose to her swollen lips. Though she'd often wondered what it would be like to kiss Dan, her fantasies hadn't come close to the real thing.

This was what had been missing when she'd kissed Steven. It was this tingle, this thrill. That didn't mean it would be wise to get involved with Dan. Amy struggled to pull *her* thoughts together. This was a major decision. One not to be made lightly.

But did she really have a choice? Now that they'd kissed, could they really ever go back to how they were before?

The clock struck one. Amy sighed and plumped up her pillow. She knew it wouldn't make a difference. Even the endless parade of imaginary sheep she'd spent the last hour visualizing hadn't helped. Try as she might Amy couldn't make herself fall asleep.

She'd told Dan they'd talk tomorrow but she still didn't have a clue what she was going to say.

If only he hadn't kissed me...

Being in his arms, feeling his mouth on hers had been incredible. When he'd acknowledged feeling something more than friendship it had been alternately a dream come true and her worst nightmare. Dan had so many good qualities. He was kind and gentle and totally devoted to those he loved. She'd seen the way he was with his wife, the way he was with Emma.

On the other hand, she remembered what happened to Bree and Melinda. The minute they'd started to care, to hope for something more permanent, to demand more than they were getting, they'd found themselves alone.

Of course, the two hadn't realized what Amy had always

known—Dan was still in love with Tess, would probably always be in love with Tess.

Amy understood what it was like to love someone who didn't love you. She'd been abandoned by her mother and left for Aunt Verna to raise.

Amy understood what it was like to want permanence. All she wanted was a home, a family and a cat. It wasn't much but at the moment her dream had never seemed more out of reach.

Amy understood that when you cause trouble, when you become demanding, you only push people away. That's why during her growing up years, she'd never given Verna one reason to get rid of her.

But Verna had relatively low expectations.

Amy wasn't sure the same could be said of Dan. After all, Bree and Melinda and the countless women before them hadn't been able to keep him happy. What made her think she could?

Perhaps Steven was right. Maybe it would be foolish to become involved with Dan.

Still, she was tempted. Despite his flaws, she was attracted to Dan. She'd been daydreaming about him, hoping he'd see her as more than just his daughter's nanny. Now that he had, could she really just walk away because she was scared?

Amy tightened her jaw. She'd never been a coward or a quitter. She was strong and smart and talented. If things didn't work out she'd survive.

It was time she took charge of her life.

It was time she fought for what she wanted.

It was time she gave Dan a chance.

CHAPTER EIGHT

"Something smells good."

Amy looked up from the griddle and smiled at Dan. "Hot-cakes. With blueberries."

Emma lifted her gaze from her plate. "An' Amy even made the syrup hot."

"Wow." Dan grinned and Amy's heart skipped a beat. "I feel like I died and went to heaven."

"I don't want you to go there." Emma's smile faded and her fork dropped to the table with a clatter. "I want you to stay here with me."

Amy's heart went out to the little girl. She reached over and ruffled Emma's hair. "Your daddy isn't going anywhere, sweetheart. It's just his way of saying he likes my hotcakes."

"Amy's right, princess." Dan dropped a kiss on Emma's head and shot Amy a grateful look before taking a seat at the table.

Amy placed a cup of steaming coffee in front of Dan but he continued to talk to Emma and didn't even look up. Even as she turned back to the stove, Amy could hear Dan's low, reassuring tone. Her heart warmed at the sight of the two heads together. By the time her own hotcakes were done and she joined them at the table, Emma was giggling.

Amy had barely taken her first sip of coffee when the school bus horn sounded. In a matter of minutes, Emma was out of her seat, racing toward the big yellow vehicle, a spring in her step and a bright smile on her face.

After making sure Emma was safely on the bus, Amy returned to the kitchen. She wasn't surprised to find Dan still at the table. His measuring look told her he'd deliberately stayed to talk. Amy knew just what he wanted to discuss.

She pretended not to notice and took her time pouring the syrup. "Big plans today?"

"I'll be in the city." He gestured with one hand as if brushing away a troublesome mosquito.

Amy forked a bit of hotcake. "It's supposed to be unseasonably warm today."

A look of exasperation crossed his face. "I don't want to talk about the weather. Not when there are more important things we need to discuss."

The impatience was so typically Dan that she had to smile.

"Oh, all right," she said in her most lofty tone, "I guess I'll give you a chance."

Surprise skittered across his face. "You will?" Amy heard the disbelief in his voice and her heart fluttered. After swallowing a piece of hotcake that seemed to have grown to the size of a baseball, Amy forced a casual, offhand tone. "Unless you didn't mean what you said. I mean if you were only joking…

"Of course it wasn't a joke," he said, seeming upset that she would even think such a thing. "I'm just surprised. I guess I was convinced you were going to turn me down."

Amy frowned.

"I'm happy you said yes," he added hastily.

"So." With one finger Amy traced an imaginary pattern on the tabletop. "Where do we go from here?"

Dan took a sip of coffee and leaned back in his seat. "How about my company party at the Palmer House Friday night?"

Amy lifted her head and met his gaze. The party, she knew, was always an elegant affair. It would either be a fabulous beginning for the two of them or a train wreck. She refused to let fear hold her back any longer.

She smiled. "It's a date."

~

The chandeliers in the ballroom of the Palmer House Hotel in downtown Chicago glittered brightly and the scent of fresh flowers filled the air.

The clink of crystal mingled with the sound of laughter and conversation. As Amy stood in the entrance to the large room and gazed out over the multitude of men in tuxedos and women in sparkly dresses, her heart lodged in her throat. What had she been thinking?

The place teemed with important people—men and women who Dan interacted with on a daily basis. Some of whom she'd met...as his nanny. She knew what they'd think when they saw her at his side. Either they'd think that Dan had lost his mind...or they'd think he was banging the nanny and she'd made him bring her.

Amy was seconds away from bolting when Dan took her hand. Her heart fluttered and she lifted her gaze.

He smiled. "I'm so happy you came with me."

"You are? Why?"

He laughed and the lines around his eyes crinkled. "Because I always have a good time when I'm with you."

The tension and anxiety, which had held Amy in a stranglehold, eased and she relaxed for the first time since they'd left the house. Dan was right. They always had fun together. Tonight would be no exception.

"Can I get you a glass of wine?" Dan stepped close, shielding her from an unsteady drunk with a loud voice and a drink in each hand.

Even after the man moved past, Dan remained close.

Amy's heart fluttered and she looked away, not wanting him to see the desire in her eyes. She smoothed the skirt of her black cocktail dress. It was the same one she'd worn when making Steven dinner, but if Dan had noticed, he'd been too polite to say a word.

Once she'd gained control of her emotions, Amy smiled "I'd love some wine. Preferably red."

Dan's gaze lingered on the tall white pillar behind Amy's back as if anchoring her place in the crowded ballroom.

"Don't move." He slanted a quick kiss across her lips. "I'll be right back."

Then, he was gone.

Amy touched a finger to her mouth and wondered if he had any idea the effect he had on her. How he made—

"Amy?" A feminine voice pulled her from her reverie. "I almost didn't recognize you. What are you doing here?"

Turning, Amy pulled her thoughts together and flashed Bree Northcott a welcoming smile. "I came with Dan."

Impulsively Amy gave the pretty blonde a hug. Bree looked fabulous as always in an emerald-green dress that showed off her lithe, model-like figure to full advantage.

A tiny frown momentarily marred Bree's brow. "I thought I heard Dan was coming alone."

"He changed his mind," Amy said in a light tone. "Who are you here with?"

According to Dan, the party was for the architectural firm and their clients. Bree worked as an attorney for a tax firm, or at least she had the last time Amy had spoken with her.

"I came with Jake," Bree said.

Amy tried hard not to show her shock. As one of Dan's closest friends, Jake had often been at the house and Amy knew him quite well. Or at least as well as she *wanted* to know him. She'd never liked the way the man looked at her—as if he was imagining her naked—or the suggestive comments he made when Dan wasn't in the room.

"He's kind of slimy." Bree lifted a shoulder in a slight shrug. "But I wanted to come to this party and he was my ticket in."

"I didn't say there was anything wrong with him," Amy said quickly.

"You didn't need to." Bree laughed. "I could see it in your eyes."

Amy nearly groaned out loud. She'd thought she'd mastered the art of keeping a poker face, but lately she'd been falling short. Way short.

"I like Jake—"

"Stop." Bree touched Amy's arm. "The guy has sex on the brain and the only thing he cares about is scoring. Please don't feel like you have to defend him to me."

"He *is* kind of slimy," Amy admitted.

"Very," Bree said with extra emphasis.

The two women laughed.

"Why did you want to come to this party so badly?" Amy asked. "I mean it's nice and all but..."

As far as Amy was concerned, a woman would have to be beyond desperate to come with Jake.

This time it was Bree's turn to shrug. "There was someone I was hoping to see here tonight, but...it's pretty hopeless. He's always had eyes for someone else."

"My, my, two beautiful ladies." Jake sidled up to Bree and leered at Amy. "Don't you look delectable."

Amy offered the man a polite smile. "Haven't seen you in a while."

"Been busy," Jake said. "Unlike Dan, I don't have someone waiting on me hand and foot when I come home at night"

Amy wasn't sure how relevant the answer was to her comment but Jake was obviously making a point. If his goal was to remind her of her place in the social hierarchy, he'd accomplished his mission.

Amy felt a tap on her shoulder and she turned. Dan moved to her side and made a great show of handing her a glass of wine. "Tonight, my dear, it's my turn to wait on you."

Though Dan's tone was light and his lips turned up in an easy smile, the tightness in his jaw told her that Dan had not found Jake's comments amusing.

She took a sip of wine and when she lifted her gaze, she found Jake blatantly staring at her cleavage and Bree staring at Dan.

Amy ignored them both and turned to Dan. "Would you like to dance?"

She didn't particularly want to show off her lack of coordination but right now she'd rather be out on the hardwood floor than standing around being ogled by Mr. Slimy.

"I'd love to." Dan placed his glass on a nearby table and held out his hand.

Amy placed her glass next to his and took his hand, smiling a goodbye to Bree. She still didn't know who Bree had come to the party to see but she had a suspicion. Yet Dan had chosen her.

The dance floor was crowded, so thankfully, Amy didn't feel conspicuous. Instead of everyone staring and pointing out her decided lack of rhythm, she and Dan were just one couple swaying to the band's beat.

"I thought you told me you didn't dance." Dan's tone was teasing and his eyes warm.

"I didn't. I mean, I don't." Amy tried to follow Dan's lead and pretend she knew what she was doing. It wasn't easy. Not only because her feet had a tendency to trip over each other but because his nearness was wreaking havoc with her self-control. Was there anything more attractive than a gorgeous man in a tuxedo? The contrast of a crisp white shirt with the dark fabric of his tuxedo coupled with his handsome face sent her heart racing.

The way he smelled... Just breathing in the spicy scent of Dan's cologne made her heart beat faster. The feel of his strong arms around her brought back memories of the last time he'd held her close. Like he was doing now.

She rested her cheek against his chest. "I lied."

This time it was Dan's turn to stumble. "What about?"

"I *have* danced before." Her heart tightened with the memory. "With my dad. He'd turn on the stereo, lift me off the floor and we'd dip and sway to the music."

"I do that with Emma sometimes."

Though she didn't lift her head and she couldn't see his face, Amy could hear the smile in his voice. "You're a good father."

"I don't know about that." Dan expelled a ragged breath. "I didn't do so well after Tess died."

She heard the emotion in his voice and her heart went out to him.

"It was tough," he admitted. "Emma reminded me so much of Tess. She still reminds me of Tess. Of what I lost"

Amy didn't even need to close her eyes to remember that time. Dan had been beside himself with shock and grief. Emma had been confused and frightened. The fact that Amy had lost a parent at a young age had helped her relate to the little girl...and to her distraught father.

"It was a difficult time for everyone." Amy kept her tone low and soothing.

"I couldn't have done it without you."

"Yes, you could," she insisted. Dan was good and strong and faced his challenges head-on.

Her own father had been such a man. After her parents had split, Amy's dad had found himself with sole custody. His love had been constant and all she'd needed. "You remind me so much of my father."

"Your father?" The look on Dan's face would have been laughable at any other time.

"Stop." Amy tugged him back to her and began dancing even as heat rose up her neck. "I just meant you're a great father. Just like my dad."

"Whew." Dan pretended to swipe some sweat from his brow. "That's a relief."

"He was a good guy." It was all Amy could think to say.

"Tell me about him," Dan said, his tone low and enticing. "I know you said he died when you were Emma's age, but I don't know much more than that." Amy hesitated. She'd spent so many years *not* talking about him that it was difficult to know where to start.

"He was wonderful," Amy said. "My mother hated him. My aunt didn't know him, but she told me to forget about the past and focus on the future."

"I can't imagine how hard it would be on Emma if anything happened to me," Dan said, almost to himself.

"Nothing is going to happen to you," Amy said quickly. "If anything does, I promise I'll do everything in my power to give Emma a happy life. You know what she means to me."

"A person doesn't have to be family to raise and love a child." A strange undercurrent wove its way through Dan's words.

"You're right," Amy said. "In fact, looking back, I'd take a stranger over my mother any day."

CHAPTER NINE

Dan pulled Amy close and let the music wash over him. She'd done it again. Without even knowing it, she had managed to reassure him that he'd chosen the right course of action.

Tess's parents were nice people but with their strong personalities and domineering ways they wouldn't be the right ones to raise his sensitive daughter. Despite what his mother-in-law believed; family *wasn't* always the best choice. Of course when he married Amy she would be family, part of *his* family. His arms tightened protectively around her. He'd make it good for her, too. She would never want for anything.

What about love?

Dan shoved the question aside. He could name a dozen couples who'd married for "love" and were now divorced. Besides, there were all sorts of love and levels of caring. While he would never lie to Amy and say he loved her when he didn't, he'd show her in every way possible he cared. Because he did care. Very much.

The band's lead singer launched into a romantic ballad and Amy snuggled close, the clean fresh scent of her hair teasing his nostrils. When she'd come down the stairs tonight, the sight of her had taken his breath away. He'd immediately noticed that she'd chosen the black dress from the other night...the one he liked so much.

For a moment he'd almost mentioned how happy he was to see it again. Just in time he'd remembered Tess's opinion on wearing the same party dress twice and had kept his mouth shut. The last thing he wanted was to hurt Amy's feelings. He couldn't imagine a dress being more perfect and he'd been proud to walk into the party with her at his side.

"Thanks again for coming with me," Dan whispered against her hair, his hand caressing her bare back.

"Thank you for the invitation." She lifted her head and smiled. "I'm enjoying myself."

"You sound surprised."

"I've never been to an event like this. I wasn't sure what to expect." Amy glanced around the room. "I have to admit I was a bit nervous."

Dan had thought as much. He'd felt the uncertainty in the hand that had clutched his arm when they'd walked into the ballroom. That's why he'd stayed close. Other than getting her a glass of wine, he hadn't ventured from her side.

When he'd come to parties with Tess, networking had been the name of the game. She'd go off in one direction and he in another. At the end of the evening they'd reconnect and maybe share a dance or two before heading home. That way of operating had become second nature and it had been the same with the women he'd dated after Tess's death. He'd never considered doing it any other way. Spend an entire evening with a woman who had nothing on her agenda except him? Dan found himself enjoying the change.

He liked being with Amy and it felt good knowing she was content just being with him.

"Ready for a trade?"

Dan turned to find Jake standing in the middle of the dance

floor, Bree at his side. For all the attention he gave her, the stat-uesque blonde might as well have been a stranger. Jake had eyes only for Amy. Or rather, for Amy's breasts.

Dan tightened his lips. He hadn't liked the way his friend's gaze had settled on Amy's cleavage earlier and he didn't like it now. She tensed in his arms and Dan could feel her heart beating wildly. It was obvious she didn't want to dance with Jake but Dan sensed she wouldn't make a scene if he agreed.

It was equally obvious Bree didn't share Amy's reluctance. She stepped forward, in anticipation of the trade.

"Sorry." Dan tightened his hold on Amy. "Tonight I'm a one-woman man."

Without another word Dan whirled Amy away and they danced off across the hardwood, leaving Bree and Jake open-mouthed and staring.

Dan could feel Amy relax in his arms. The tense look that had blanketed her features eased.

"One-woman man?" A giggle punctuated Amy's words. "I can't believe you said that. It sounds like a title to a country song."

Dan grinned. The relief in her eyes told him he'd made the right decision.

"I meant every word," he said. "Tonight I'm all yours. And you're all mine."

∽

You're all mine.

The raw emotion in Dan's voice sent a thrill up Amy's spine. She'd never wanted to "belong" to any man, but tonight she found herself enjoying the feeling of being cherished and protected.

When Jake had wanted to change partners Amy had frozen, like a deer trapped in a headlight's glow. The last thing she'd wanted was to be within ten feet of Jake—much less in his arms—

but how could she voice that sentiment knowing Jake and Dan were friends? Especially with Jake standing right there.

She needn't have worried. Dan had taken control and Amy seriously doubted Jake would ask again. She heaved a contented sigh. This evening was quickly falling into the category of events that she would remember forever. Amy didn't have many such memories, which made tonight even more special.

"You know what I'd like to do?" Amy abruptly lifted her head and gazed into Dan's eyes.

He wiggled his eyebrows. "Dance with Jake?"

"Um, no." Amy tried to keep her expression serious but his lighthearted teasing made that impossible. "I'd like a picture."

Dan's company had hired several photographers to provide guests with mementos of the evening's festivities. They'd set up a couple of stations in the ballroom and had been busy snapping pictures all night. The backdrop of fresh flowers they were using reminded Amy of something you'd see in prom pictures. Not that she had firsthand knowledge. When Amy had been in high school, she'd never gone to any of the dances. There hadn't been money in her aunt's house for fancy party dresses. Instead Amy had worked those nights, waiting tables, serving her fellow classmates.

Still, it wasn't as if she looked back on that time with regret. Except...she'd secretly longed for a picture of herself all dressed up with a handsome male at her side.

"Pictures?" Dan's gaze shifted to the nearest photographer who was just finishing up with a gray-haired couple.

The doubt in his eyes told her he wasn't keen on the idea. Feeling gauche and unsophisticated, Amy quickly rallied, offering up a little laugh, pretending she'd only been joking. "I just thought it might be fun to show Emma. But you're right. It's a crazy idea."

Crazy or not, Amy couldn't keep her gaze from glancing in the direction of the camera one last time. She expected Dan to take the out she'd offered, but when she turned back to him he hesitated, his gaze lingering on her face.

"I don't think it sounds crazy at all. I think it sounds like...fun," he said, his eyes clear and very, very blue. A slight smile lifted his lips. "Kind of deja vu-ish...like high school."

Amy's heart gave an excited leap, but she forced a nonchalant tone. "That's kind of what I was thinking."

The rest of the evening raced by. Amy got her picture taken with Dan—despite some ribbing from Jake, which Dan squelched with a single glance— then danced some more.

Amy's intuition had been right. Jake didn't ask to exchange partners again. Amy kept an eye on Bree and discovered the woman's gaze seemed to be permanently fixed on Dan, a sad look in her eyes. Amy now knew exactly who Bree had come to see.

By the time they were ready to leave, it was after midnight. Amy stood off to the side, while Dan retrieved her shawl. Though normally she'd be in bed by now, Amy wasn't the least bit tired.

She glanced at the pictures in her hand. The photographer had instructed her to face Dan and place her hands flat against his chest. After she'd done as he'd asked, he'd positioned Dan's hands on her waist. Amy had been drowning in the deep blue of Dan's eyes when the photographer had snapped the picture...

"Are you ready?"

Amy's head jerked up. Dan stood in front of her, holding out her shawl. He was looking at her, not with the blatant invitation she often saw in men's eyes, but with a combination of unmistakable interest mixed with a hint of uncertainty.

Amy shoved the photo back into the decorative folder and let him wrap the silky fabric around her. She glanced down at her watch. If she could believe her former classmates, a milestone evening was considered a failure if you went home before dawn. It was barely past midnight. "You know, don't you, that if this *was* prom night, we'd never be going home this early." Like Cinderella faced with turning back into a scullery maid, Amy hated the thought of the evening ending so soon. They could at least grab a bite to eat and talk over a cup of coffee. "Want to stop somewhere on our way home?"

"Sounds good to me." Dan's eyes darkened. "I'm definitely in the mood."

His comment didn't make much sense until they were in the car and Dan started talking about the make-out point in his town.

"It was on a hill." His lips curved upward in remembrance. "Overlooked a lake. The view couldn't be beat, not that we spent much time gazing at the moon." Amy's smile froze. Dan wasn't planning to stop for a burger. No, thanks to her ambiguous question, they were going to park.

Her body turned hot then cold at the thought of locking lips with Dan in the warm intimacy of the car.

"How about you?" Dan asked. "Where did *you* go?"

Amy took a steadying breath and wondered what he would say if she admitted that the only place she'd gone on prom night was back to her aunt's apartment after a grueling shift at the restaurant.

She had her pride. She couldn't let him know she'd been such a nerd. Her mind raced. Other than renting rooms at the hotel where the dance had been held, she couldn't recall any of her classmates mentioning a specific place they'd gone to park. "Mostly back roads. No place specific."

Dan turned off the highway onto a residential street. "A deserted road it is."

Amy's heart skipped a beat. She glanced out the window. The night was dark with only a sliver of moon. Large trees lined both sides of the road, their large, leafy branches arching overhead, creating an air of intimacy in the vehicle passing below.

It wasn't long until the row of houses gave way to farmland and pavement turned to gravel. Still Dan continued to drive.

"How far are we going?" Amy asked.

"Not much farther." Dan shot her a sideways glance. "Just enough so we won't be disturbed. Of course, I seem to recall it was that fear of discovery that made the experience so exciting."

His wicked smile fired her blood and for a second she forgot to breathe.

Dan wheeled the car to a stop at the side of the road, flipped off the ignition and the lights.

"This was a good suggestion." Dan's voice was soft and low in the stillness. "I was hoping we could go somewhere after the dance."

"You were?" Though Amy tried to keep her voice casual and offhand, it came out breathless and a whole octave higher than normal.

Dan nodded. "Once we got home I knew there'd be no privacy."

Amy knew he was right. Emma was a light sleeper. Odds were the little girl would be up and down the stairs before the baby-sitter was out the door. But they weren't in Dan's house. They were in the car. Alone. Just the two of them.

Feeling like a nervous schoolgirl, Amy shifted in the seat and faced him. A curious thrumming filled her body.

"I'm not sure my aunt would approve of me being here alone with you." She shot him a saucy smile. If she'd been seventeen, Amy had no doubt she might have said something very similar.

"I've got an idea." Dan tugged her wrap from her shoulders and flung it into the back seat. "Let's not tell her."

Though the temperature inside the car was comfortably warm, Amy's skin turned to gooseflesh. She'd meant the teasing words as a joke and had been unprepared to have him play along.

Heat pooled low in Amy's belly and she decided if Dan was interested in being seventeen for the night, she would go along.

"I'm not sure I can trust you." Amy crossed her arms over her chest and stuck out her bottom lip. "I've been warned about boys like you. You only want one thing."

"That's not true." Dan's voice remained sensuously soft and low. He trailed a finger up her arm leaving a flash of heat in its wake. "I don't want just *one* thing...I want lots of things."

His crooked smile was endearing but there was something in his tone, in the underlying seriousness lurking behind the playfulness that set up a fluttering in her stomach. He studied her for several seconds and she found herself holding her breath. "I'd like to kiss you," he said finally. "Is that okay?"

Amy chewed on her lip and tilted her head, pretending to ponder the question. "I suppose...as long as you don't try any of that fancy French stuff."

"You don't like to French kiss?"

The shock in his voice made Amy smile. She wasn't sure if it was the teenage Dan or the adult who was most distressed.

"I've never tried it." Amy clasped her hands primly in her lap like a virginal teen. "Aunt Verna says that kind of kissing is bad."

Amy had never discussed such a topic with her guardian, but she couldn't imagine Verna thinking anything else.

"Hmm." Dan slipped an arm around Amy's shoulder and nudged her to him. "I don't want to contradict the woman but French kissing is very good. Don't take my word for it. Give it a try. Then decide for yourself."

His arms closed around her. "I want you to know that I would never do anything to hurt you."

Amy's body was now pressed so tight against Dan that she could feel the heat radiating from his body. She drew a calming breath only to find herself immersed in the rich, spicy scent of his cologne. With her heart pounding, Amy moistened her lips with the tip of her tongue. "I know—"

The words had barely left her lips when his mouth closed over hers. Slow and sweet the kiss teased and tantalized and the desire Amy had held in check broke forth and surged through her veins like a raging river.

She slid her fingers into his soft hair, pulling him closer, the uncontrollable fire burning inside her demanding more than slow and sweet. Dan's hands remained respectfully at her waist and his kisses, while intoxicatingly sensual, remained close-mouthed and chaste.

When his lips left hers to scatter kisses along her jawline and neck, Amy groaned with frustration. He was doing as she asked, but couldn't he tell she'd changed her mind? Dear God, did she have to spell it out to him?

His lips reached the curve of her neckline then moved back up.

Amy decided she'd had enough. A woman could only endure so much frustration. "I changed my mind."

His mouth paused on her neck. He lifted his head. "You want me to stop?"

"Yes." When he pulled back, Amy realized with sudden horror what she'd just said. "No. I mean I want you to move on."

Amy knew she wasn't making much sense. But could she really be expected to think rationally with his warm breath caressing her neck?

"Move on?" He lifted a brow. "I don't understand."

"I want you to kiss me. *Really* kiss me."

The puzzled look in his eyes told Amy she still wasn't making herself clear.

"Ooh-la-la," Amy said, her French accent worthy of a kinder-gartener. *"Comprenez-vous?"*

The dimple in his cheek flashed. "But your aunt—"

"Screw my aunt."

Dan's lips quirked upward but he wisely withheld comment. "Anything else you'd like me to do?"

"Maybe," she murmured, glancing up at him through lowered lashes.

"You want it." Pure male satisfaction filled his tone. A high school boy couldn't have sounded more proud.

No need to define what *it* was. She'd experienced *it* on more than one occasion and though the experiences had hardly been memorable, having sex wasn't something a woman forgot.

"Nice girls don't go all the way," Amy said, sticking to her virgin persona. "I just want to kiss...maybe fool around a little."

Even in the darkness, Amy saw Dan smile.

"So everything but." Dan pretended to mull over the idea. Finally he nodded. "That still gives us a lot of territory to cover."

"Depends," Amy said, being deliberately vague, keeping her options open. "I might decide to stop with French kissing."

"I don't think so."

The arrogant undertone raised her ire. She sniffed. "Don't be so sure."

His gaze dropped. "What about these?" Unexpectedly Dan reached forward and brushed the silky fabric of her bodice with the back of his knuckles. Her nipples instantly hardened beneath his touch. Amy gasped.

"Think how much fun it would be—" his voice turned deep and seductive "—if this dress wasn't in the way."

Amy didn't even have to close her eyes to visualize the erotic scene. With her dress out of the way, he would be free to use his mouth and hands to the fullest.

Her breasts strained against the silky fabric and an ache filled the juncture of her thighs. She craved and wanted this man in a way that defied logic. Still, being half-naked in a car with a randy male was something a teenager might do, not a responsible adult. Yet, she couldn't quite bring herself to refuse. As if Dan could sense her wavering, his lips closed over hers.

"Please." He spoke softly against her mouth. "It's prom night. We're not children. We can do what we want."

Amy had never been much of a rebel. The wildest thing she'd ever done was to dance in a conga line at a local bar on a friend's twenty-first birthday.

We can do what we want.

It was prom night. Or as close to prom night as she was ever going to get.

He deepened the kiss and Amy welcomed the moist heat and slow, penetrating slide of his tongue. A purr of passion rumbled in her throat. Dan was an irresistible temptation and the kiss made her hungry and restless for more of him.

She wouldn't sleep with him. That would be just plain foolish. *Everything but* held a certain decadent appeal. Amy turned in her seat and offered him the back of her dress. "Unzip me, please."

CHAPTER TEN

Unzip her?

The moment the words left Amy's lips, part of her wanted to laugh and pretend she'd only been joking. The other part, the part that wanted, no, *needed* to feel his hands on her body kept silent, waiting for Dan to make the next move.

For half a heartbeat Dan hesitated as if he, too, realized the enormity of the step they were taking. Then his hand moved to the zipper and the back of her dress eased open.

Amy's skin turned to gooseflesh and anticipation skittered up her spine. While she didn't expect Dan to go caveman on her, she did expect things to start moving. But Dan didn't seem in any hurry.

After what seemed an eternity, he placed a lingering, open-mouthed kiss on the back of her neck. The mere touch of his smooth, moist lips sent blood surging through her body. Amy closed her eyes and exhaled a ragged breath. This was definitely a good start.

Now, if only the dress was off...

Despite knowing it would only take the slightest of shrugs to drop the silky garment to her waist, Amy waited. As eager as she was for some skin-to-skin action, she was a traditionalist. Old-fashioned to the core, Amy liked the man to take the lead. But when Dan placed his hand against her back, Amy jerked upright and stiffened, her reaction more like a high school sophomore who'd never been touched than a mature woman.

"Relax," he said in a low soothing voice, rubbing his palm lightly over her skin.

Amy's face burned with embarrassment and she opened her mouth. Once his hand settled on her back, she found it difficult to breathe, much less talk.

His fingers were strong, yet gentle and her entire body tingled at his touch. Warm shivers of sheer pleasure coursed through her veins.

"Mmm," she sighed. Had she died and gone to heaven? It seemed entirely possible.

"Want me to continue?" His deep voice held a teasing lilt.

"Mmm-hmm," was all Amy could manage.

Thankfully Dan understood what she wanted.

While scattering kisses across her shoulders and up her neck he continued to gently move his hand over her lower back. With each slow stroke, each unhurried touch, her desire grew. When he slid his hand upward, she moaned softly and arched her spine against him.

He played her like a fine violin, drawing her out, making her respond as she'd never responded before. The darkness and solitude inside the car lent a dreamlike air and Amy wasn't sure what part of this wonderful experience was fantasy and what was reality. Whichever it was, one thing was certain—she didn't want it to end.

"That feels incredible," she said, exhaling a long breath. She desperately wanted Dan to keep touching her. Her breasts ached to be touched and lower, between her thighs, she felt a heavy warmth and a dull throb.

His hand slipped deeper inside the dress and curved around

her waist. Slowly and ever so sensuously, his hands slid upward until his fingertips were no more than an inch from the underside of her breast.

Breath held, eyes closed, Amy quivered with anticipation. She felt him lean close, felt the warmth of his breath on her shoulder, felt him gently turn her in the seat so she faced him. Her eyes fluttered open and excitement coursed through her when she saw the gleam in his eyes. There was a promise there, one that said there was more, much more to come.

"You are so beautiful." His voice was soft and gentle as a caress.

Though she knew he was only being kind, Amy loved the way the words sounded on his lips. She wished she were beautiful. For herself. For him.

Dan saw the wistful longing in Amy's eyes and he vowed that by the end of the evening she'd believe his words. He'd make her *feel* beautiful.

A warm rush of emotion filled him. Amy was such a good person. So kind. So sweet. So incredibly sexy.

He raised a hand and cupped her face. Lowering his head, he pressed his mouth against hers. He ran his tongue over the fullness of her lower lip, coaxing her to open to him, sweeping inside when she did. She tasted of wine and breath mint, a ridiculous combination that was wildly erotic.

She curled her fingers into the fabric of his shirt and leaned into the kiss, her tongue fencing with his. The slow, delicious thrust and slide brought his body to high alert.

Her skin was like warm silk beneath his fingers and Dan fought the urge to slide his palm upward and feel the firm weight of her breast in his hand. He reminded himself there was no reason to rush. They had all the time in the—

A light flashed and a sharp rap sounded on the window.

"Sheriff's deputy," a deep voice announced. "Everything okay in there?"

Amy jerked back, her eyes, which had been heavy-lidded with passion, suddenly wide-open. "Police."

Dan whirled in his seat and stifled a curse. Despite the outside darkness and his vehicle's tinted windows, he could still see the uniformed officer and the flashing lights.

"I need you to step out of the car," the man ordered.

"I'll take care of this." Dan flashed Amy what he hoped was a reassuring smile, pushed open the door and stepped out into the cruiser's spotlight "What seems to be the problem, Officer...Wayne?"

Though it had been almost five years since he'd seen Wayne Bojanski, Dan recognized him immediately. Wayne had been his buddy in grade school, a casual friend in junior high and a football teammate at Barrington High.

"Dan Major?" A grin of recognition split Wayne's ruddy face. "I never thought I'd find you and Tess gettin' frisky on a country road."

Dan's smile faded as the realization hit. Wayne didn't know about Tess. He'd last seen Wayne at their ten-year high school reunion and back then Tess had been very much alive.

Dan didn't even need to close his eyes to remember the evening. That night had been classic Tess. She'd been laughing, dancing up a storm and charming everyone in sight. It all seemed so long ago and Dan was surprised to find that the memories of Tess didn't hurt as they had before.

"Tess died three years ago," Dan said finally as the silence lengthened.

Wayne's eyes widened. His mouth dropped open. "You're kidding."

Yeah, Dan wanted to say, I'm kidding, she's really alive. But he understood Wayne's comment was just an expression of his shock and disbelief.

"It was sudden," Dan said. "A medical problem."

Wayne pulled his mouth shut and cleared his throat. "So then, who's in the car?"

Dan blinked, the blunt question catching him off guard. "A friend." Normally cool and collected in any circumstance, Dan found himself stammering. "We had some things to discuss and wanted some privacy."

"Friend? Discussion?" The deputy's lips twitched. "C'mon, Dan. This is ole Wayne you're talking to..."

Dan couldn't help but smile. Okay, so maybe his explanation was pretty lame. He probably should just admit he and Amy had been parking. After all, Wayne and his wife, Tami, had spent more than their fair share of time locking lips—and doing God knows what else—in the back of Wayne's old Buick.

The words wouldn't come. Something in Dan wouldn't let him joke about it with Wayne. He couldn't shrug off the feeling that by doing so, he'd cheapen what he and Amy had shared.

"It's quiet out here," Dan repeated, lifting his chin and meeting Wayne's gaze head-on. "Not many distractions."

"Good for discussions," Wayne added, barely able to keep a straight face.

"Is this going to take much longer?" Amy's voice came from inside the Land Rover.

Wayne's face broke into a grin and a devilish gleam lit his eyes.

"You can go now. I'm sure you and your friend have a lot to *discuss*." Wayne placed an arm companionably around Dan's shoulder and lowered his voice. "You just have to do it somewhere else."

Dan couldn't speak for Amy, but for him dirt roads no longer held any appeal.

"Don't worry," Dan said. "You won't see me around here again."

Wayne glanced at the car then back at Dan. "One more thing—"

Dan wished he could just jump in the Land Rover and speed away. He remembered that tone. Wayne had always considered himself to be an expert on women. He loved to offer his own kinky brand of relationship advice. Dan braced himself.

"I'm sorry to hear about Tess." Wayne kicked the gravel with the tip of his boot. "I liked her. She was spunky."

Dan's heart stuttered, the unexpected sentiment taking him by surprise. He silently accepted the condolence. Dan appreciated Wayne's words. But he didn't want to talk about Tess tonight or even think about her. This evening was about the future, not the past.

The deputy wasn't even in his cruiser when Dan pulled away from the side of the road and cast a sideways glance at Amy. "Thanks for getting things moving back there. Wayne will talk forever if you let him."

Amy's lips quirked upward. "I guessed as much."

"I'm sorry about that." Dan gestured toward the darkness. "I didn't plan on the cops showing up." Though his gaze was on the road, Dan sensed Amy's scrutiny.

"You knew him," she said simply.

"Wayne and I go way back...to kindergarten. We played football together in high school." Dan kept his tone deliberately light. "The guy always did have bad timing."

"It was probably for the best," Amy said in a matter-of-fact tone. "I have the feeling things would have gotten out of hand."

"That would have been a...bad thing?"

Amy chuckled and Dan felt the tension ease from his shoulders. At least he could still make her laugh.

"I'll definitely remember tonight." Her lips twitched. "A girl always remembers her first time." Startled, Dan's brows shot up.

"The first time—" Amy's smile widened "—I was ever busted by the cops."

When she began to laugh, he laughed along with her. Her eyes shone like the finest emeralds and the enticing scent of her perfume wafted around him. All he wanted to do was pull over and take up where they'd left off. But Dan wasn't seventeen. He was an adult and wise enough to realize they'd been lucky. Five or ten minutes later and Wayne would have gotten an eyeful.

No, a car was *not* the place for a romantic interlude with Amy. There were plenty of other options they could explore.

"Tonight was definitely an evening to remember," Dan said. "Care to go out again and make some more memories?"

Amy lifted a finger to her lips and thought for a moment. "As long as the memory doesn't involve law enforcement or dirt roads."

Though he agreed wholeheartedly, Dan couldn't resist a little teasing. "Where's your spirit of adventure?"

"Oh, I can be very adventurous." Amy shot him a sultry look from beneath lowered lashes and Dan's mouth went dry. "It's just that when I'm kissing someone, I don't want to worry about being interrupted. . .especially not by the police."

Impulsively Dan reached over, grabbed her hand and brought it to his lips.

"Next time there won't be any interruptions," he said. "I guarantee it."

No interruptions.

Unable to sleep, Amy stared up at the ceiling of her bedroom. When she and Dan had walked through the front door, their time alone had come to an abrupt end.

Dan had done his best. He'd kept his voice low and hurriedly paid the sitter. Emma must have had her "Daddy radar" on because Dan had barely ushered the baby-sitter out the front door when Emma came running down the stairs.

The child's appearance had brought reality back with a vengeance. Amy was once again the nanny and Dan was, well, Emma's daddy and her employer. While Amy understood—and completely agreed with—the need for discretion around Emma, she still felt like a child whose favorite toy had been snatched from her hands.

Amy's fingers rose to her mouth as the disappointment resurfaced. She hadn't even gotten a good-night kiss. Unless you counted the ones in the car, that is. A smile touched her lips. She never realized parking could be so much...fun.

Dan certainly knew how to kiss. When he held her in his arms and his lips closed over hers it was as if nothing else in the world existed. It was—

A familiar melody rang out from the cell phone on her nightstand and Amy jerked upright. She glanced at the clock and frowned: 2:00 a.m. Why would Steven be calling at this hour?

Amy considered letting the call go to voice mail but curiosity got the better of her. She grabbed the phone and flipped it open. "Hello."

"Amy." Even across the airwaves she could hear the surprise in his voice. "I didn't expect you to answer. I was just going to leave a message."

While Amy wasn't used to getting calls at this hour, she welcomed the distraction. Maybe talking to Steven would take her mind off Dan and help her relax. "I usually shut off the ringer but I guess I forgot."

"I'm sorry I woke you."

His distress was palpable and Amy hastened to reassure him. "You didn't. I was lying here looking up at the ceiling, trying to decide if I should count sheep or get up and read when you called."

"I've had trouble sleeping, too," Steven said in a low, husky timbre. "I wanted to hear your voice, even if it was just a recording."

Warning bells sounded in Amy's head. She liked Steven but the truth was, she hadn't given him much thought since he'd been gone. Of course if it had been Dan who'd been out of town...

"—fly here."

Amy's fingers tightened around the phone. She realized with sudden horror that while her mind had been wandering, Steven had continued to talk. The question was, about what?

"Fly to Boston?" Amy asked, slowly, cautiously.

"I want you with me," Steven said in that take- charge way that was as much a part of him as his hand- tailored suits. "My days are booked, but you could shop or sightsee. We'd have evenings together."

Amy couldn't help but be flattered that he'd want to spend his free moments with her. Steven was a handsome man, a successful attorney...not to mention a fabulous cook. He had a lot to offer a woman.

Even if she was interested, there was no way she could go.

"You forget I have a job." She deliberately gentled her tone wanting him to understand she appreciated the offer even if she couldn't accept "It's impossible for me to get away."

"Amy." She could almost see Steven shaking his head. "Dan Major can find someone else to watch his daughter and clean up after him for a week."

"I'm sure he could," Amy said, feeling a pang of distress at the thought. "I was actually referring to the Chez Gladines business."

Getting this chance to show off her talents was a major accomplishment for an untried chef. Amy wasn't about to let the opportunity slip away before she'd proven herself.

"I have this job on a trial basis," Amy explained. "Keeping it is very important to me."

"I understand." Admiration filled Steven's voice. And something else. Something that sounded like relief. "That job is your first step toward true independence."

Amy pulled her brows together. "I've been on my own since I was eighteen."

Silence filled the phone line for several seconds.

"Don't take this wrong, but you really *haven't* been independent. Not in the truest sense of the word." Once Steven got started he seemed to warm to the topic. "You went from your aunt's home to your first nanny job and from there to your current position."

Amy's heart picked up speed and irritation warmed her face.

"You make it sound like I've been mooching off these people," she said. "I work hard for the salary I receive. Just because free room and board is part of my fringe benefits, that doesn't mean I'm not independent"

Steven had definitely hit a nerve. From the time Amy had been small she'd been determined to be self-sufficient She was not going to end up like her mother, depending on a man to "take care" of her.

"You have so many talents, Amy," Steven said. "I just want to make sure you take the chance to develop them."

Amy's anger fled, replaced by curiosity. "Why do you care?"

"Because I like you."

It was a logical answer but there was something in his voice, some element of restraint that told Amy this went beyond a pat answer. "There's more to it than that."

After a moment of silence, Steven spoke. "My mother worked for years as an administrative assistant for a wealthy Chicago industrialist. She was a smart woman with a lot of talent but he refused to promote her. Having her around met *his* needs."

Amy leaned back. "What happened?"

"He decided it was in his best interest to move to France last year." Steven's voice tightened. "Now she's in her late fifties and back pounding the pavement."

Amy could appreciate Steven being protective of his mother but it sounded as if she'd made a choice to stay in the job. Just like Amy had. "She could have gotten another job at any point. Couldn't she?"

"Of course," Steven said. "But he constantly told her how important she was to him, how they were a team...until he no longer needed her. He used her, Amy. I don't want to see that happen to you."

The degree of bitterness in Steven's voice startled her.

"Still—"

"Think about it," Steven said, his voice low and tight. "If Dan remarries, the new wife might decide she wants you gone and just like that you're history."

"I don't think Dan—"

"He doesn't even have to remarry," Steven continued. "What happens when Emma gets older? Goes off to college? All I'm asking is that you don't make the same mistake my mother did. Make yourself and *your* dreams a priority while you're still young and capable."

Amy sank deeper into her pillow, a sense of emptiness creeping over her. She could see why Steven was effective in the courtroom. He was passionate and very persuasive.

"Amy? Are you still there?"

"I'm here." She forced the words past a sudden tightness in her throat. When she'd graduated from high school, there had been no money for further schooling. Being a nanny had started as a temporary solution, a way to support herself while she attended cooking school at night.

She'd completed her courses shortly before arriving at the Major household. Then Tess died and Amy couldn't leave Dan and Emma then. But did that mean she had to spend the next ten or fifteen years standing off to the side watching Dan and Emma live their lives but never *really* being a part of their world? Even after tonight, what if their relationship didn't move forward? What if Dan married someone else?

She thought she'd stayed with the Majors out of love for Emma, but was that simply an excuse? Had she stayed out of fear instead? Or for Dan?

"Are you angry?" Concern filled Steven's voice.

Amy took a deep, steadying breath. Her inner turmoil was *her* problem, not his. "No. I'm sure you only want the best for me."

"I do." His voice took on urgency. "I care—"

"Listen, Steven, I'd love to talk more but I need to get to sleep." Amy had enough on her mind. She couldn't deal with what she feared could be a declaration from Steven.

"May I call you tomorrow?"

"Of course."

"One last suggestion." Steven spoke quickly as if he sensed she was ready to end the call. "Don't get personally involved with Dan. It'll just make leaving his household that much harder when the time comes."

When, not if.

Amy's heart twisted. The warning had come a little too late. "I'll keep that in mind. Good night, Steven."

"Sweet dreams."

Amy clicked off the phone. Sweet dreams? Was he kidding? She had so much to think about she'd be lucky if she slept at all.

CHAPTER ELEVEN

Amy rose the next morning, pulled on her clothes and headed to the kitchen. She told herself she'd been foolish to spend half the night worrying over her budding relationship with Dan. She was different than Bree and Melinda and her situation was nothing like that of Steven's mother. Steven had his own agenda and it obviously included coming between her and Dan. Well, Amy wasn't going to let that happen.

The sound of talk radio came from the kitchen. Amy paused in the doorway and all her doubts slipped away. Dan sat at the table reading the paper.

He looked up when she entered the room. Even with his hair still mussed from sleep and a slight shadow darkening his cheeks, he still made her heart skip a beat. "Hey."

"Hey, yourself." Amy returned his smile and, instead of moving to the coffeemaker, she pulled out a chair and took a seat at the table. "You're up early."

Dan lowered the paper to the table.

"Couldn't sleep," he said, closing his hand over hers. "Someone was on my mind."

Amy willed herself not to blush. Still her cheeks warmed. "Yeah, right."

"I'm serious." Dan's eyes twinkled. He looked more devilish than serious. "You didn't even give me a good-night kiss."

A warm flush of pleasure washed over Amy. So she wasn't the only one who'd felt cheated.

"Emma was there," Amy said in a light tone. "We could hardly kiss in front of her."

Dan looked around the room, his movements exaggerated. "I don't see her now."

Amy's gaze never left his. "I checked on her before I came down. She was fast asleep."

"We saw last night how quickly that can change." Still holding Amy's hand, Dan pushed back his chair and stood.

Amy followed his lead. "Are you saying there's no time to waste?"

Even as Amy said the words, he pulled her to him. "Oh, yeah."

A brush fire of heat sizzled through her as he lowered his head.

His lips brushed softly over hers, once, twice with a teasing gentleness. Parting her lips, Amy touched her tongue to his bottom lip. In a heartbeat the kiss changed.

With a low groan, Dan wrapped his arms more firmly around her. His mouth covered hers. She was completely surrounded by him, by the delicious feel of his body against hers. Warmth emanated from his skin. His large hands combed through her hair then slowly skimmed down her back. She reciprocated but went a step further, tugging his shirt from the waistband, slipping her hands inside.

Desire, hot and insistent, gushed through her. She ran her palms up his back, reveling in the contrast of smooth, firm skin over hard muscle. Everything faded except the need to feel more of him. Taste more of him. Touch more of him.

Logic told her to slow down but unfortunately logic wasn't in charge. Besides, he was having none of it and she wasn't about to argue.

He lowered his head and ran kisses down her neck. She arched back. A low groan escaped her as his lips dipped lower.

"A-my." The childish voice coming from the top of the stairs broke through the fog of arousal engulfing her. "I can't find my pink shirt. Do you know where it is?"

Apparently equally startled, Dan froze, lifting his head

Amy cleared her throat. She knew exactly where to find the garment, but she didn't want Emma downstairs any sooner than necessary. "I'll be up in a minute to help you look."

Pulling in a much-needed deep breath, Amy returned her attention to Dan and found him studying her with enough simmering heat to melt a polar ice cap. "That was some good-night kiss," he said finally.

She swallowed. "It was okay."

"Okay?" The dimple in his cheek flashed. "Only okay means we'll have to keep practicing."

A wealth of emotion rose inside Amy, surprising her with its intensity. No longer could she lie and tell herself she thought of Dan as merely a friend. He turned her on by just being in the same room. His kisses had more kick than, well, than anything she could think of. But it was Dan, who he was, what he stood for, his wit, his charm, that drew her to him.

She'd tried to keep her heart safe but every look, every smile, pushed her a little closer to the edge. She only wished she could be certain that if she went over that edge...he'd be there to catch her.

Dan pushed open the front door and headed down the steps. Once he reached the sidewalk he turned left. Bagels and Jam was only three blocks away. Hot, fresh blueberry bagels had been his getaway excuse. He'd felt the need to put some distance between him and this unsettling woman who had all but turned him into one big, pulsating hormone. His reaction to her bordered on embarrassing.

God knew he'd been ready to devour her in the kitchen. When she'd first walked into the room with her shiny hair tumbling around her shoulders in a tangle of curls, every one of his nerve endings had jumped to attention. She obviously hadn't taken the time to apply any makeup because a spray of delightful freckles marched across her nose. She looked fresh, clean and good enough to eat.

If Emma hadn't gotten up when she had, Dan didn't doubt for a second that things in the kitchen would have quickly burned out of control. While Amy seemed willing, he didn't want to rush her into something she might regret.

Last night and this morning had told him the attraction was there. While he couldn't imagine loving her like he loved Tess; lack of passion wouldn't be an issue.

Dan found himself distracted as he pushed open the door to the shop. The place was surprisingly busy. He stood at the end of the line behind an attractive woman with salt-and-pepper hair who looked vaguely familiar. He must have caught her eye when he came in because she turned, a spark of recognition lighting her gaze.

"Aren't you Dan Major?" she asked.

"I am." Dan's mind raced. He tried to place her but no name was forthcoming. He was just about to admit that fact when she stuck out her hand.

"Angela Bartgate," she said. "My late husband Tom and I used to live two doors down from you on Deming."

"Of course." Dan's hand closed over hers. Now he understood why he hadn't remembered her. They'd only met once or twice. She and her husband had left the neighborhood shortly after Dan and Tess had moved in. "You moved to...Wisconsin?"

Angela nodded. "Our daughter lives in Madison. We wanted to be closer to her." A shadow passed over the woman's face. 'Tom was getting ready to retire. He never got the chance. He was killed by a drunk driver six months ago."

The woman's voice thickened. She blinked rapidly for several seconds.

Dan's heart went out to her. Though he'd only met her husband once, Dan knew firsthand what it was like to lose a spouse.

"I can understand what you're going through," he said. "My wife, Tess, died three years ago."

The woman's eyes widened with shock and sympathy filled her gaze. "Oh, my goodness, no. What happened?"

"Are you two ready to order?"

The bored voice seemed to come out of nowhere and Dan realized with a start they'd reached the counter. They ordered and made light conversation while they waited. When their drinks and food were ready Dan reached for his wallet "These will be together."

Angela glanced up at him. "You don't have to do that."

"I know." Dan handed the man behind the counter a twenty. "I want to do it."

"Would you like to sit and have a cup of coffee with me?" Though Angela's voice remained calm and composed, the hopefulness in her eyes spoke of desperation. "I'm visiting friends down the street and they both like to sleep late. Tom and I were both early risers. Mornings are still hard for me."

Dan thought for a moment. Amy and Emma would have plenty to do until he got back.

"Sure," Dan said. "I'd love the company."

It wasn't true, of course. He'd walked down here specifically for the solitude. To reflect on what had happened last night and again this morning. But Angela's pain was almost palpable and Dan remembered how lonely he'd been when Tess had first died.

He couldn't begin to imagine how much worse it would have been if not for Amy.

"Looks like there's a table by the window," Angela said.

Dan was determined to keep the conversation light, but the minute they sat down, the woman leaned forward and rested her hand on his forearm.

"I'm so sorry to hear about your wife," she said. "What happened?"

Dan shifted uncomfortably in his seat. While thoughts of Tess no longer sent waves of pain crashing over him, he still didn't like talking about that time. Short of being rude, he didn't see that he had any other choice.

"Tess was pregnant with our second child." Opening a packet of raw sugar, Dan dumped the granules into his cup. "There were complications. She and the baby died."

"How heartbreaking." Tears filled Angela's eyes. "I still remember the first time we met. It was a glorious fall day. Tom and I were working in the yard. You and Tess were pushing your daughter around the block."

Dan remembered that day, too. Emma had been fussy. He'd put her in the stroller, planning to give Tess a break so she could work on a new design that was giving her trouble. At the last minute Tess had insisted on coming with them.

"You two were so much in love." Angela's eyes grew misty. "Just like Tom and I."

Dan took a sip of coffee, not really tasting it. "It seems like such a long time ago."

"I assume you still live in the same house?"

It was a logical assumption. After all, she'd run into him just down the street from where she'd once lived. "Still there."

Angela broke off a piece of scone but made no attempt to eat it. A curious glint lit her eyes. "Have you remarried?"

"No," Dan said. "It's difficult to think of being married to anyone but Tess..."

Dan let his voice trail off as he added another packet of sugar to his coffee. He took a sip and grimaced at the sweetness.

"My friends tell me I'm too young to spend the rest of my life alone." Angela stared down into her latte for a moment before lifting her gaze. "But Tom was my soul mate. I'm never going to find anyone I'll love like that again."

The image of Tess flashed before him. Spiky blond hair. Big blue eyes. An enchanting smile. She'd been his first love. From the time he'd been a boy, his only love.

Then another image intruded. One of caramel-colored hair, bright green eyes and a sprinkling of freckles.

Tess had been wonderful, a real gem. But as time went on Dan was finding it impossible to think of Amy as second best to anyone.

He wrapped his fingers around the coffee cup, the warmth a vivid contrast to his suddenly cold hands. "I've considered marrying again. Emma needs a mother and I, well, it'd be nice to have a companion."

The minute the word left his mouth, Dan knew it was all wrong. Companion conjured up images of a buddy, not an emerald-eyed temptress who made his day brighter by simply being in the same room.

"Still, I'm not sure it's fair to marry if you're not in love," he added before he could stop himself.

Normally Dan wouldn't consider discussing an issue of a personal nature with a stranger. But then, Angela wasn't a part of his daily life and he couldn't—wouldn't—air this concern with anyone he might see again.

Certainly not with his mother who'd tell him he needed to be honest with Amy. Or with Jake who'd tell him flat out to do what was best for *Dan* and not worry about the nanny.

Dan wasn't sure what he wanted from Angela, unless maybe it was for her to validate that marrying him would be a good thing for Amy. *Even if romantic love wasn't part of the equation.*

Angela took a bite of scone and chewed thoughtfully. "I think we'd both be surprised at how many people marry for reasons that have little to do with love."

"I can see where it could happen," Dan said. "Take my situation for example. I have a child that could really use a mother and I can't imagine spending the next fifty years of my life alone. Still, is settling the right thing to do?"

Was marrying Amy settling? He preferred to think of it as—

"I can understand not wanting to be alone." Angela stirred her latte and her brows furrowed.

"It could be a win-win situation. Marriage could be a good thing for her, too," Dan inserted before she could continue, feeling like a lawyer presenting a case, desperate to get all the evidence in before a verdict is rendered. "I could give her the life she's always wanted."

"That might work," Angela said, but the doubt in her voice sent unease creeping up Dan's spine. "As long as—"

Dan kept his face expressionless, hoping she couldn't hear the pounding of his heart. He lifted a brow.

"As long as the life she's always wanted never included a man who loves her."

Dan leaned back in his desk chair and stared unseeingly at the computer monitor. He'd come back from the bagel place, edgy and out of sorts. While he'd been able to keep his emotions under control, it had still been a relief when Amy had left to take Emma to dance class.

Angela had given him a lot to think about. Dan grimaced. He'd never thought he'd be in this predicament. He'd never thought his wife would die young. He'd never thought he'd have to worry about what would happen to his daughter should a similar fate befall him.

"Dan?"

He turned in his chair.

Amy stood in the doorway, a glass tumbler filled with iced tea in one hand. "I thought you might be thirsty."

Dan glanced at the clock, surprised to discover so much time had passed. He hadn't even heard her return. "How was the dance class?"

Amy smiled. "They're practicing for the *Nutcracker.* Emma is so excited. She's just a Snow Angel but you'd think she had the lead."

Although the finer points of ballet escaped him, Dan liked watching his daughter jump and spin. He smiled and, obviously taking the gesture as a sign of real interest, Amy went into more detail about the lesson. When she started throwing around technical ballet terms she lost him.

If this was important to Emma, then it should be important to Dan. He knew he should be focusing on the tale she was weaving, but Amy's red lips made it impossible for him to concentrate. The freshly applied color made her lips look plump and juicy, like the most delectable of strawberries. Recent experience had taught him that those lips *tasted* as good as they *looked.*

Dan's gaze dropped to take in the sight of her distracting curves and long legs. There was a lump in his throat, a mixture of lust and fear and something else he couldn't identify. Dear God, what was happening to him? The woman stops in to offer him some tea and talk about his child and all he can think about is jumping her?

Or was focusing on the physical attraction that simmered between them a way to keep from thinking about other, deeper issues?

"Dan?"

He blinked and realized she'd quit talking.

"Is something wrong?"

"No." He shook his head. "Fifth place and pivots. Fascinating stuff."

A tiny smile hovered on the edges of her lips. "It's fifth *position* and *pirouettes* she corrected. "And I can tell something is on your mind."

Without waiting for an invitation, she crossed the room, placed the tea on a coaster at the edge of the desktop and took a seat. "What's going on? Spill."

What's going on is that I want to marry you because I need a mother for my daughter and a companion for myself but now I'm not sure that'd be fair to you.

A look of distress filled her gaze and for a second Dan worried he'd spoken his thoughts aloud. Then he realized it was his silence she was reacting to, not to any words. His mind quickly searched for a plausible excuse for his inattention. "I was wondering about Thanksgiving."

An expression he couldn't decipher flickered in her eyes. "I hadn't thought much about it."

Dan couldn't hide his surprise. Although Amy had holidays off, they'd always spent them together. She'd always gotten into the holiday spirit way before the actual day, planning menus and what they could do to make the day special for Emma. Of course, that was before Steven.

"I hoped you'd spend the day with us," Dan said. "Unless you have plans with someone else?"

A startled look crossed her face before her eyes grew shuttered.

"I sort of thought I'd stick around here." Her gaze lowered to the desktop and her finger traced an imaginary pattern on the glass.

Relief flowed through Dan. He couldn't imagine spending the day with anyone else. She'd been a big part of his Thanksgiving for the past three years.

The first year she'd single-handedly prepared a meal for him and Tess and a houseful of guests. The next year Tess was gone and Dan had no interest in entertaining. Though he'd told her not to bother, Amy had made dinner and insisted he sit down and eat. Every year she'd outdone herself.

Impulsively Dan rose, rounded the desk and took a seat in the chair next to her. Taking her hand, he gently caressed her palm with his thumb.

"I can't imagine spending Thanksgiving with anyone but you." His gaze remained riveted to hers. "You're the one I want with me. Understand?"

Amy entwined her fingers with his. The deep blue of his eyes drew her in and she found herself slipping from the firm shore of what she'd always known to a place where she could be over her head in an instant.

She wanted him and when he tugged her to him, she went willingly, eagerly. While he hadn't yet said he loved her, he'd come close. That was good enough for now.

Dan raked his fingers through his hair, grateful for Emma's nonstop chatter beside him as they walked to the park.

You're the one I want with me.

Even to his ears the words sounded like a declaration.

After his talk with Angela, Dan had vowed that he would not mislead Amy about his feelings. If she committed to him it would be based on the friendship and trust that existed between them— not because he implied he was in love with her.

Because he wasn't in love with her. Tess had been his soul mate and everyone knew you only got one of those.

"Amy's making a booberry pie for Thanksgiving," Emma said. "I don't think I've ever had that kind. Have you, Daddy? Is it good?"

Dan pulled his thoughts to the present and to his little girl. He smiled down at her and love welled up inside him. "I have and it's very good. Especially with ice cream."

"I can't wait for Thanksgiving." Emma did a little dance on the sidewalk. "Amy makes everything good."

Dan wasn't sure if his daughter was talking about merely the food or the atmosphere. Either way, he had to agree.

He cast aside any lingering doubts and solidified his decision to marry her. She'd be a good wife. A wonderful mother. A passionate lover. He'd do everything in his power to make her happy.

Now all he had to do was get her to say yes.

CHAPTER TWELVE

Amy glanced at the clock on her dashboard and pressed harder on the accelerator. Dan had taken Emma for a walk while she'd finished her French pastries. Dropping them off at Chez Gladines had taken longer than she'd planned. Now she was late. After so many years in the school system, Aunt Verna didn't tolerate tardiness well.

Amy had been looking forward to puttering around the house, finishing a few projects and most of all just spending the day with Dan and Emma. But Verna was in town and wanted to see her. How could she say no?

She'd thought she was meeting her aunt at a restaurant for coffee. But the address Verna gave her led her to a brick home in Lincolnshire. If Aunt Verna's Buick hadn't been in the driveway, she'd have thought she was at the wrong place.

Amy glanced at the piece of paper on the seat next to her, then back at the numbers on the mailbox. That was the address she'd been given. That *was* her aunt's car. So, this must be the place.

In less than a minute, Amy stood on the front stoop, listening to the ring of the doorbell echoing through the house. The door opened and relief flowed through Amy at the sight of her aunt

Verna stood in the doorway, ramrod stiff, her lips pursed together. "You're late."

The bluntness was typical Verna. Her aunt had never been a subtle woman. Sugarcoating was something only done to cookies. Still, over the years Amy and her aunt had bonded and she'd come to love the taciturn woman.

"Well, are you going to stand there staring, or are you going to give me a hug?" The words shot from Verna's lips like a bullet.

Amy laughed and wrapped her arms around Verna's stiff shoulders. "I've missed you."

The hug only lasted a second before Verna pulled away, her voice brusque. "Now that we've given the neighbors plenty to talk about, come inside and I'll show you the place."

Amy followed her aunt into a large living room with a fireplace across the far wall. Other than Verna's sofa and love seat, there wasn't much else in the way of furniture. Several cardboard boxes sat in the middle of the floor. The place had a definite just-moved-in feel to it.

She turned to her aunt. "Is this yours?"

Verna's lips curved slightly upward. "Mine and the mortgage company's."

"I didn't know you were that serious about moving." Amy tried to keep the hurt from her voice. She couldn't believe her aunt had bought a house and moved without telling her.

"It dropped in my lap," Verna said. "My friend decided to participate in a teacher exchange program with a school in Germany. Her kids are grown and she plans to buy a town house when she returns."

"I never thought you'd leave Mankato." Amy remembered how active Verna had been in the small Minnesota community. "You knew practically everyone in town."

"I've got friends here." Verna ushered Amy into the kitchen.

Amy's smile faded.

"And family," Verna added hastily.

Amy resisted the urge to sigh. While deep in her heart she knew her aunt loved her, she'd always felt more like an obligation. That was part of the reason she was so determined to marry for love. She wanted the man she married to be as crazy about her as she was about him. For once, she wanted to come first in someone's life.

"Have a seat," Verna ordered, gesturing toward an oak pedestal table already set for tea. "We'll have tea and cookies before I show you around."

Amy sat down and, with typical Verna efficiency, the tea was soon in her cup and several cookies on her plate.

'Tell me what you've been up to." Verna nibbled on a shortbread cookie, a curious glint lighting her eyes. "Are you dating anyone?"

"I've gone out a few times with a guy I met in my cooking club," Amy said. "He's nice."

Nice. Not special. Not like Dan.

If she and her aunt were confidants, Amy would have mentioned Dan, maybe even sought her aunt's advice. But Verna had never really made an attempt to get to know Dan, despite Amy's repeated tries.

Verna lifted a perfectly tweezed brow. "Are you spending Thanksgiving with him?"

"Steven hasn't asked," Amy said. "If he did I'd have to say no. I'm cooking dinner for Dan and Emma."

"Working on Thanksgiving?" Verna's mouth drew together in disapproval. "Surely that man can spare you for one day."

Amy's spine stiffened and she dropped her cookie back to the plate. Aunt Verna and Steven always made it sound like Dan was some sort of ogre when nothing could be further from the truth. Emma and Dan were like family. She *wanted* to celebrate the holidays with them.

"He'd give me the day off if I asked him," Amy said, unable to keep the indignation from her voice. "I love to cook and holidays are a big deal for Emma—."

Verna's eyes flashed. "It's also a time for you to be with your family."

Amy suddenly realized this wasn't about Dan. This was about Verna. For the last five or six years her aunt had spent Thanksgiving in Texas with a close friend and her family. Buying the house must have put her in a bind and now she was facing a holiday alone.

Reaching across the table Amy covered her aunt's hand with her own. "Come and spend Thanksgiving with us. I know Dan would love to see you again."

"You talk like it's your house," Verna said in a no-nonsense tone. "He's your *employer*, Amy, not your husband."

Amy's cheeks burned as if she'd been slapped. "I know who he is, Aunt Verna."

Her words were as measured and clipped as her aunt's had been.

"I didn't mean to make you angry." Verna's eyes were clear and direct. "I'm worried about you."

Amy gave a little laugh. "Worried? Why?"

Verna's gaze never wavered. "You're twenty-eight years old. It's time you had a family of your own."

"But—"

"Hear me out." Verna raised a hand. "I know you enjoy being that child's nanny, but you're not getting any younger. It's time you started thinking of yourself. Started thinking what it is you want out of life."

I want Dan.

Amy kept her mouth closed. She already knew what her aunt would say if she mentioned her daydreams about Dan, about how she hoped they could one day be a family. Verna would tell her she needed to be realistic, to see life as it was, not how she wished it would be.

"I love Emma," Amy said instead. "She and Dan are like family."

"You've been there too long," Verna said. "You're too attached."

She was attached. For the past three years Dan and Emma had been her family. The three of them had spent every holiday together. Not just holidays. She'd been there to celebrate Emma's birthday...and Dan's. And they'd celebrated hers.

Amy took a sip of tea, met her aunt's gaze and took the plunge. "Lately Dan has been making noises like he'd like to date me. Maybe see where things could go between us."

Verna closed her eyes and visibly shuddered. "A recipe for disaster."

"Maybe not," Amy said. "We've always gotten along so well."

"Because you're his employee," Verna said. "You wait on that man hand and foot."

"I do—" Amy started to protest then stopped herself. Her lips curved up in a rueful smile. "Okay, I'll admit it. I like to pamper him."

Verna didn't even crack a smile.

'That's precisely why you get along so well." Verna stabbed the air with one finger for extra emphasis. "He says jump, you ask how high."

"You forget taking care of him and Emma is my job," Amy protested.

"What about those other women he's dated?" Verna asked. "I seem to recall you telling me that everything was fine until they started making demands."

"That was different."

"How?" Verna pressed. "Has he mentioned love?"

Amy rubbed the bridge of her nose between her thumb and forefingers, feeling a headache coming on. "It's just different."

Verna leaned forward and took Amy's hands in hers. This time there was only kindness and caring in her gaze. "Forget the fantasy. Make a life for yourself. Find someone who truly cares about you...and what you want. Do it now. Before it's too late."

~

Amy drove home from Verna's, feeling irritable and out of sorts. While she told herself that her aunt didn't know what she was talking about, Verna's comments played on her deepest fears.

Was she crazy to think that Dan could really love her when she'd witnessed firsthand his love for Tess? Had her own desire blinded her to the reality of the situation?

The problem was she couldn't deny that Steven and her aunt had an advantage she didn't. They could step back and make a judgment based on fact, not emotion.

By the time Amy pulled into the garage, she'd convinced herself she'd been foolish to think Dan could ever care for her in a 'til-death-do-us-part kind of way. Hadn't she seen how it had gone with Bree and Melinda? He was in between women and he found her attractive. Period. End of story.

She shut off the ignition, not sure whether to be sad or happy to see Dan's Land Rover in the garage. She needed to end their short-lived relationship. If things went any further, it would be impossible for her to stay.

She wanted to stay. On this subject Verna was wrong. There was no reason she couldn't continue to build her catering business while taking care of Emma and Dan. Regardless of what anyone else thought, Amy could not just walk out of Emma's life. Amy knew what it was like to lose someone you loved. She knew what it was like to feel abandoned. She knew what it was like to feel alone in the world.

Emma isn't alone. Emma has Dan.

Amy shoved the thought aside. Maybe she *was* staying for herself but there was absolutely no reason she couldn't have a full and complete life of her own *and* care for Emma. First she had to set some limits on her relationship with Dan.

She walked into the house fully prepared to do just that only to discover he wasn't home. A note on the kitchen told her Emma was spending the weekend with a friend but said nothing of Dan's whereabouts. Amy only knew that with his car in the garage, he had to be close.

Tension knotted her shoulders and the headache that had hovered on the edge of her consciousness at her aunt's house began to pound in her temples. Swallowing a couple of Tylenol, Amy headed upstairs to relax for a few minutes.

After locking the door to her suite of rooms, she stripped off her clothes and padded into the bathroom, the soothing jets of the whirlpool tub calling to her. She wasn't sure how long she relaxed in the scented water, listening to music, but by the time she got out her headache was barely noticeable.

She considered getting dressed and doing a little housework but quickly discarded that notion. After all, this was her day off. So instead, Amy picked up a book to read. Almost randomly, she chose a popular romance and the magic of the book propelled her to her bed, where she spent the next hour propped up against her pillows reading.

She was halfway through the book when her ringing phone jarred her from the pages. Still lost in the story, she answered absently. "This is Amy."

"Amy, this is Philippe from Chez Gladines." The confident masculine voice held the faintest hint of a French accent. "How are you this evening?"

"I'm fine." Amy managed to get out the words without stammering. Other than her initial job interview, she hadn't had a lot of contact with Philippe.

"Your pastries are *tres magnifique,*" Philippe said. "Very popular with the customers."

Amy relaxed her death grip on the phone. "You called to—"

"I called to offer you a full-time job," Philippe said. "I'd like you to take over all the desserts and pastries at the restaurant."

"I still have two months left of my trial period," Amy said.

"You have already proven yourself." Philippe's decisive tone brought home the reality of the offer. "Come in on Monday and we'll discuss salary and benefits. If you're interested, that is."

"I am interested." Amy's head spun. Being a fulltime chef at a place like Chez Gladines had been a pie- in-the-sky dream. Now the position was being handed to her on a silver platter.

The only problem was this job wouldn't work with her nanny position. "I do have another full-time job but I will most certainly consider your offer. I could be there around one on Monday?"

"I'll see you then," Philippe said. "And, Amy—"

"Yes, Philippe?"

"I really hope you take it."

Amy clicked off the phone and sat there, stunned. Several of the waiters had mentioned how well her desserts had been selling, but she'd never thought it would lead to a permanent position.

What about Dan and Emma? Her heart twisted. Dan paid her to take care of Emma and the house. How could she possibly do both jobs at once? Lots of women do, a tiny voice in her head whispered. Tess had a demanding career and a family. But Tess, Amy reminded herself, was Dan's wife, not an employee.

Amy pressed her fingers against suddenly throbbing temples. Dear God, why did her life have to be so complicated?

She gave herself a sudden shake. This was ridiculous. Tonight was her night off. She refused to ruin the evening by obsessing over the negative. She'd get a bottle of wine, have a couple of glasses to celebrate the offer and finish the book she'd been reading. She'd think about all the implications tomorrow.

Grabbing the chenille robe from the foot of the bed, Amy pulled it on over the boxer shorts and tank top and cinched the belt tight around her. She dropped the book into the pocket.

After sliding her feet in a pair of tiger-striped mules, she headed down the stairs.

By the time she reached the main floor, the throbbing at her temples had reached bongo drum proportions. She stopped in the kitchen and found some ibuprofen in the bottom of her purse. Swallowing a couple, she glanced at the clock. She'd give the pills a half hour. If two didn't help, she'd up the dosage to prescription strength.

She pulled a bottle of wine from the rack, hoping a little Merlot might be just what the doctor ordered. By the time she'd poured herself a glass, the long flight of stairs to her room held little appeal. She decided to stay on the main level and relax in the parlor.

The renovated parlor had terrific ambiance not to mention a chaise lounge and a fireplace. Though the robe Amy had on was thick and fluffy, the air in the house held a definite chill. The thought of basking in the warmth of a gas log suddenly seemed irresistible.

In a matter of minutes she sat on the chaise, a fire burning brightly in the hearth. Even with a wineglass in one hand and her book in the other, Amy found it difficult to concentrate.

Despite her determination, her thoughts drifted to the decisions she faced and she couldn't focus.

Her heart tightened and a few tears slipped down her cheeks. How could she leave Emma? She couldn't love the little girl any more if she was her own daughter. And how could she tell Dan goodbye?

Darn it, this wasn't fair. To realize one dream, she had to give up another? Or did she? Tess had been a career woman. Would Dan support her?

The pounding in her head increased and despite knowing it would only make things worse, Amy couldn't help herself. She began to cry.

CHAPTER THIRTEEN

After walking Emma to her friend's house, Dan stayed to admire their recent renovation work. When the football game came on, it seemed rude *not* to stay and have a beer. As the sun set, he realized it was time to head home. Ted invited him to stay for supper but Dan had other plans for the evening.

When he got close to home, a light in the parlor window beckoned and he quickened his pace. He wondered if Amy would be interested in going out tonight. Maybe they could take in a movie. With Steven still gone, she shouldn't have other plans.

His jaw clenched at the thought of the arrogant lawyer but he reminded himself that he was taking care of that situation. By the time Steven returned, Amy would be his fiancé.

Dan pushed open the back door, expecting to find Amy in the kitchen. That room was as empty and silent as the dining room. He was in the hallway when he heard her. His heart stilled in his chest at the plaintive sound.

He hurried to the parlor. She looked up when he entered the room, hastily brushing aside her tears. Though Dan told himself that if something bad had happened, she'd have called him, fear still gripped him in a stranglehold.

"Is it Emma?" Dan could barely get the words out. How something could happen in the short time it had taken him to walk home, he didn't know. All Dan knew was he'd never seen Amy this shaken. "Did Ted or Abigail call?"

"No." Amy drew a shaky breath and forced a smile. "They didn't."

Relief flowed through him, but then he realized something still had upset Amy. If it didn't involve his daughter...

Dan's heart softened at the look of distress furrowing her brow. He found himself wanting to kiss and make whatever was bothering her all better. Even after what they'd shared, pulling her into his arms seemed too familiar a gesture. He settled for moving across the room and taking a seat next to her on the chaise. "Tell me what's wrong."

"It's nothing." She smiled. "I just have a lot on my mind."

If not for the fact that she rarely cried, he might have believed her. His mind raced as he tried to figure out what might have upset her. She'd been in good spirits when she'd left the house this morning. His gaze narrowed. "You went to see your aunt."

She looked down at her hands for a moment before lifting her gaze.

"She only wants what's best for me." Amy pressed her fingers against her temple. "Everyone only wants what's best for me."

Dan forced a light tone. "What is that?"

"It doesn't matter." She closed her eyes briefly and exhaled a ragged breath, then rose to her feet. "My head really hurts. I'm going to bed."

Now that she mentioned it, he could see the lines of strain around her eyes.

Dan stood, put an arm around Amy's shoulder and steered her out in the hall toward the stairs. "Get into bed and I'll bring you some warm milk."

Amy scrunched up her nose.

"You don't like warm milk?"

She shook her head then winced at the movement "Not so much."

"Come to think of it, neither do I." Dan smiled ruefully. Hot milk had been his mother's "cure for all that ails you."

It had been the first thing that had popped into his head. He decided it was more appropriate for insomnia than for a headache. "How about some aspirin? Extra-strength Tylenol?"

"There's some ibuprofen in the kitchen cupboard." Amy's gaze shifted down the long hall. "I could take a couple more."

"I'll find the bottle and bring them up."

Amy turned to him and laid her hand flat against his cheek, her eyes soft and luminous. "Thank you for being so nice to me."

His skin tingled beneath her touch and he was tempted to capture her hand and kiss her palm. This, he reminded himself, wasn't about *his* wants and needs, it was about making Amy feel better.

"Don't worry about a thing," he said. "That headache is as good as gone."

Amy climbed the stairs, her feet as heavy as lead weights. Crying had brought her headache back with a vengeance. When she reached her room, Amy headed straight for the feather bed. She threw off her robe and slid beneath the covers. Even as she told herself to relax, her mind returned to her dilemma.

She wanted the job but she wanted Dan and Emma, too. She already knew what Aunt Verna and Steven would say. They didn't understand. Dan wasn't simply her employer; he was her friend. He cared about her. She cared about him...

"Here you go."

Amy looked up to find Dan standing next to the bed, tray in hand. Instead of just a pill bottle and water, there were two cups of tea and a plate of cheese and crackers.

Placing the tray on a side table, Dan handed her the pills and water.

Amy sat up, popped two tiny tablets into her mouth and washed them down. Although she'd been careful not to move too quickly, the pounding in her head exploded. She winced and brought her fingers to her temples.

"Here." Dan took a seat on the edge of the bed. "Let me do that."

He sat so close Amy could feel the heat from his body. "That's okay. I'm—"

"Stubborn," he interjected, his teasing smile taking the sting from the word. His fingers brushed hers aside and he slowly began to massage her temples.

"Humor me," he said in a low, soothing tone. "I want to help. I've been told I'm quite good at this sort of thing."

After several minutes, the pounding in her head eased. Some of the relief was due to the pills and the wine. Some was definitely due to Dan's magic fingers. She sighed. "That feels good."

"You're so tense." Dan's brows furrowed. "Let me see if I can get rid of some of this tightness."

His hands moved to her shoulders. Kneading the muscles between his strong fingers, he worked on the knots until she sighed with relief.

When his fingers slid beneath the spaghetti straps of her top to focus on her shoulders, it hit Amy that she was *naked* beneath the shirt.

She shivered.

"Why don't you lie down?" he said. "You can cover up and get warm and I'll massage your neck."

"You don't have to."

Dan placed a finger over her lips, stilling her words. "If you say that one more time—I'm going to have to—"

Kiss you. Amy silently filled in the blank before abruptly turning on her stomach. She found herself oddly disappointed when he pulled the sheet up past her waist.

"Do you have any lotion?" he asked.

"On the dresser."

He was back in a second and, after rubbing the lotion between his palms to warm it, his fingers went to work on her shoulders.

No massage Amy had ever experienced before had affected her in this way. The others had been administered by strangers, licensed professionals. Not by Dan who made her heart beat faster by just walking into a room.

"If you want, you can rub my back, too," Amy said.

His hands momentarily stilled on her neck and she wasn't sure which of them was more surprised by her boldness.

"Unless you don't want to," she said hurriedly.

"No, that's fine," he said in a casual tone. "Do you want me to do it over the sheet? Or... ?"

Amy chewed on her lip. Dare she voice her true preference? Oh, what the heck.

"If you're going to use lotion, it'll have to be skin." Amy kept her tone nonchalant as if they were discussing the night's dinner menu instead of him putting his hands inside her shirt.

"Skin it is." Dan pulled the sheet back to her waist and his hands slid beneath her shirt.

Amy swallowed a gasp.

His hands moved against her skin, slid up her arms, across her shoulders, then down her back. It was the softest, most tantalizing sensation, made more so by the knowledge that it was Dan touching her with such care, such firm strength.

Her nipples tingled and an ache of wanting made her squirm. Each time his fingers traveled down the side of her body, Amy found herself hoping he'd take a detour to the front. But he was a perfect gentleman. After several minutes Amy was ready to scream with frustration.

He was being kind.

He was being solicitous.

He was driving her crazy.

Amy wanted more, but she wasn't sure if asking for more was wise. After all, there were so many good reasons to remain lying on her stomach pretending this was simply a back rub.

When he leaned close and pressed a kiss against the back of her neck, she'd had enough. Without giving herself a chance to think twice, Amy flipped over. "I think I need a total body massage in order to completely relax."

It was as bold a statement as she'd ever dared to make but to her relief her cheeks remained cool. Dan's gaze met hers. She could see surprise in his eyes, but there was something else there as well. A spark of hot desire that told her she wasn't the only one who wanted more.

The knowledge made her bolder still. She forced a teasing tone. "Unless you're too tired? Or maybe you have a headache?"

He shot her a wink. "I think I have enough stamina to go the distance."

The distance. Amy's mouth went dry.

"What about *your* headache?"

"Headache?" Amy blinked and realized the throb had disappeared. "All gone."

"Great." Dan leaned close and brushed her lips with his.

The shadows had deepened and the bedside lamp bathed them in a golden glow, creating a private little world, a tiny island of glowing beauty with just the two of them in it.

Dan's lips moved down and he was soon exploring the soft skin behind her ears and down her neck, his mouth open against her, as his hands massaged her shoulders, her arms.

"Does that feel good?" he murmured.

"Oh, yes." She exhaled the words. "Now instead of being cold, I'm hot."

His eyes darkened. "I want you to be comfortable."

Dan hooked the spaghetti strap of her T with one finger. "Less clothes might help."

"How about you?" Amy swallowed past suddenly dry lips. "Aren't you hot?"

Dan didn't answer. Instead he sat up, quickly unbuttoned his shirt and shrugged it off then shot her an expectant gaze.

Without taking her gaze off his muscular chest, Amy yanked her tank top over her head and sent it sailing across the room.

For a long moment Dan simply stared. "You're so beautiful," he said. "I could look at you forever."

"More," she said, although if pressed she couldn't have said whether she wanted him to touch her or say more pretty things.

Every part of her longed for his touch, his caress. Just when she thought she was going to faint with anticipation, he cupped her breasts in his hands, gliding his thumbs over her aroused nipples.

She moaned low and deep, and grasping his hair in her fists, she tugged his head down. He appeared to know instinctively what she wanted, burying his face between the soft fullness of her breasts. His teeth scraped over one perfect swell followed by a slow, wet, luxurious lap of his tongue.

Amy gasped in delight, her fingers biting into the muscles of his upper arms as she arched her back, silently begging him for more.

Opening his mouth wide, he suckled her hard and deep and laved her nipple with the flat of his tongue.

She closed her eyes and gave into the sensations racking her body. Yes, oh yes, this was what she'd longed for. This was what she'd dreamed about

She couldn't keep still. Her hips lifted, she laced her fingers through his hair, encouraging him as he continued. The world seemed distant, dissolved, and Amy was aware of only the two of them as he gave her the intimacy her body and soul craved.

His fingers closed around the top of her silky boxers, which were on the floor in a matter of seconds.

Amy lifted her gaze, her pulse skittering at the blue fire in his eyes. No man had ever looked at her with such hunger, such desire. No matter how much he wanted her, it couldn't come close to how much she wanted *him*. She hooked her fingers around his waistband.

"Off," she demanded.

She didn't have to ask twice. His pants and his boxer briefs landed in a heap somewhere behind him, and he stood before her, in all his naked glory.

Her eyes widened. Her tongue moistened suddenly dry lips. She knew she was staring but she couldn't help herself. He was so big. Broad shoulders. Large hands. Huge...

"Amy." The single, husky-voiced word sounded faintly like a question.

She wanted to reply, to say his name but she could only open her arms to him. He came to her then, leaning her back against the pillows, the breadth of his shoulders spreading her legs wider.

When he pressed his open mouth against the sensitive skin of her inner thigh, Amy nearly jumped off the bed. The sight of his dark head between her legs, the brush of his tongue dampening her flesh brought a deep groan to her throat.

"You smell so good," he whispered, his warm breath caressing her. "Like flowers."

He blazed kisses all the way up her leg, across her belly, then moved away, leaving her quivering with need while he grabbed a tiny foil packet from the wallet in his pants' pocket and readied himself for her.

Amy stilled at the brush of his erection against her. For the first time she felt fear nip at the shimmering edge of arousal. It had been so long. He was so...magnificent.

He must have sensed her hesitation because he stopped. "If you're not sure..."

She could see his need, his desire, on his stunning face, in his brilliant eyes.

This was Dan, she reminded herself shoving aside any doubts, and she trusted him. She wound her arms tightly around his shoulders and wrapped her legs over his.

"I want you." Amy lifted herself up, moving her hips against his in a sensual rhythm as old as time.

Desire swamped caution as need, raw and wild, returned to consume them both. The urgency built, higher, hotter, then broke fiercely inside her, his name on her lips when she clawed his back and shattered. His hands on her hips, he held her tightly, his thrusts deep and hard, fast. On a groan, he shuddered violently, again and again.

When he stilled, she slid her arms around his neck and drew him close. The weight of his body pressed her into the mattress. Smiling, Amy sank into the softness and brought him with her.

"I'm crushing you," Dan said when he could think again, when he could breathe. His heart was still thundering in his head, his lungs burning.

"No." Amy tightened her hold on him. "Don't move."

Dan couldn't have moved if his life depended on it No experience had ever left him this spent, this weak. It took all he had to lift his head and gaze down at her.

Her face was flushed, her hair a damp tangle on her cheeks. As he watched, a single tear slipped free, tracing a silvery path across her temple before disappearing into the caramel-colored softness of her hair.

His heart contracted. "Amy?"

Her lashes lifted slowly.

"Are you okay?" he asked quietly. "Did I hurt you?"

"Yes. No. I—" She lifted an unsteady hand to touch his face. "Thank you."

He grabbed her hand and pressed it against his mouth. "The pleasure was all mine."

"It was incredible," Amy said, still looking dazed.

"If you ever need another back rub..." Dan let his voice trail off and shot her a wicked grin.

Her laughter created all sorts of interesting sensations, none of them having anything to do with humor. Dan groaned, swallowing her gasp as he began to harden inside her.

"Again," he whispered.

Shivering, her hands clinging to his shoulders, Amy gave him what they both wanted.

CHAPTER FOURTEEN

Amy woke before dawn, not certain she could move, let alone get out of bed.

The pillow under her head was crooked, half stuffed under the headboard. The bed was a mess, covers pulled loose and twisted, her plush down comforter on the floor. She had the vague memory of Dan pulling the top sheet over both of them but it now lay pooled at her feet.

Still, she wasn't cold.

Her gaze slid to the man sleeping soundly beside her. He lay sprawled on his stomach, one arm thrown across her body, his hand resting just below her bare breast, fingers open and relaxed.

Dan had been an amazing lover. Tender and gentle one moment, then lusty and demanding the next. Amy had only been with two other men and with both of them she'd been a passive participant.

Not last night. Her gaze lingered on the thin red lines on his shoulder blades from her fingernails.

Such loss of control wasn't like her. She was quiet. Reserved. According to her last boyfriend, undersexed. She wasn't the type of woman who left marks of passion on a man's back. Not the sort of woman who ever had moments of passion, for that matter.

Her gaze lingered on Dan's sleeping face. He looked younger in sleep, some indefinable tension gone. She still couldn't believe Dan was here with her. The man she cared for, the man she felt achingly close to, the man she loved...

Amy stilled as the reality washed over her. Despite her best efforts to keep her heart safe, she'd given it to Dan. While Amy desperately wanted to believe he felt as she did, she knew better than to confuse the physical act of making love with the emotional feeling of love.

Yes, it would be very foolish indeed to read too much into what happened last night. For now, just being close would have to be enough.

Amy cuddled up next to Dan and let her eyelids drift shut.

Dan stared at Amy's sleeping form. Last night had blown him away. Though it'd be easy to put what had happened between them down to just great sex, he knew what they'd shared went beyond the mere physical.

There had been a connection between him and Amy. When they'd touched, the trust they had in each other allowed for no reservations, no awkwardness. As the caresses had become more hurried, more desperate, a wealth of unexpected emotion had risen up in him.

Just looking at her now, so innocent, so vulnerable, made him want to pull her close and protect her. No one could take care of her the way he could. No one would be as good to her as he would. No one.

Amy stirred, murmuring something he couldn't understand before snuggling into the pillow. A strand of hair lay curled against her cheek. Dan's fingers itched to tuck it behind her ear. But he knew it wouldn't stop there.

He'd already kept her up half the night and if he stayed in bed much longer, he'd end up waking her so they could make love again. He'd never experienced anyone like Amy before. He wanted to experience her again. And again. But she looked so peaceful that he didn't have the heart to disturb her. Casting one last regretful glance at his sleeping beauty, Dan retrieved his clothes from the floor and crept out of the room.

Dan normally kept his showers short, but this morning he found himself standing under the warm spray, trying to make sense of his tangled emotions.

He lifted his chin and let the water beat against his face. He could no longer deny it. His feelings for Amy went beyond friendship. While he didn't want to call what he was feeling love, he knew he cared deeply for her. Their lovemaking had made him realize just how empty and hollow his life would be without her in it.

It was time. Time to move forward. To make Amy a permanent part of his life. To formally ask her to marry him.

She wants your love, a tiny voice deep inside niggled. Amy deserves to be with a man who loves her.

Dan shoved the voice aside. Amy deserved to be with the man *she loved.* All the signs last night said that was him.

His mind returned to the task at hand. Before he could propose he needed a ring. Dan thought for a moment.

Grandmother's engagement ring.

His initial impulse was to discard the notion. It lingered. Dan had never been quite sure why Gram had left the ring to him. At the time, Tess already had a square-cut diamond solitaire set in glittery platinum, a ring as hip and modern as Tess herself. His grandmother's ring, with its ornate old-world charm and intricate scrollwork, would have been totally wrong for her.

Not for Amy.

Amy was a traditionalist whose jewelry and clothing reflected a kinder, gentler time. Dan's lips curved upward. The diamond had been locked in the parlor safe for almost six years. It was time it saw the light of day.

~

Sunlight streamed through the windows, warming Amy's face. She rolled over, her outstretched arms finding only an empty bed. Her eyes popped open.

Surely I didn't imagine...

Amy sat up and the covers fell away. The cool air turned her bare skin to gooseflesh. She shivered and pulled the sheet up to her chin, a wry smile tipping her lips. No, last night hadn't been a dream.

She had a sudden memory of looking into the mirror and seeing Dan's naked back, muscles rippling as he moved over her. No, the kisses, the caresses, the unquenchable heat had been very real.

The evening had been a revelation. She'd always respected Dan. She'd always liked Dan. Last night she'd realized she *loved* Dan. Though it sounded goofy— and she'd never say it aloud— when they'd come together, Amy had felt as if she was finally whole.

"Amy?"

She lifted her gaze. The object of her affection stood in the doorway; his face freshly shaven with hair still slightly damp from the shower. He was also...fully clothed.

Disappointment coursed through Amy. It might be broad daylight. They may have just made love only a few hours earlier but she wanted him naked and back in her bed.

"I wondered where you'd gone." Her casual tone was at odds with her racing heart.

"There was something I needed to do," he said with a slight

smile. His gaze dropped to the sheet now wrapped tightly across her chest.

Amy's nipples hardened. As his gaze lingered, every nerve ending inside her began to buzz. She was tempted to let the sheet drop and see if she could entice him out of those clothes. Somehow, without her quite realizing how it had happened, she'd somehow made the leap from shy prude to wanton woman.

"Mind if I sit down?" he asked in a sexy voice that slid through her like fine wine.

"Not at all." Amy scooted over, letting the sheet drop ever so slightly.

His gaze didn't leave her face.

Get a grip, she scolded herself. Last night was fun and games. Today, it's business as usual.

"Have you thought about what you want for lunch?" Amy tucked the sheet firmly around her. "I've got leftover roast beef and some Swiss—"

Dan closed her lips with his finger. "We can deal with food later."

His gaze grew thoughtful. "I've been thinking about last night. You just didn't seem like yourself."

Amy's blood went cold. If this was about all her loud moans she was going to pull the pillow over her head and never come up for air. She'd never been vocal during sex before. She hadn't been able to help herself. Not when Dan possessed an uncanny knack for finding the most sensitive spots on her body.

"You seemed...distracted," he added.

Distracted? Hardly. From the instant his hand had settled on her skin, he'd had her full attention. Her face must have reflected her surprise because Dan smiled.

"Before the back rub," he clarified. "You'd been crying."

Amy didn't want to remember what had been on her mind before she'd lost herself in his touch. It all came rushing back. Aunt Verna's blunt comments. The phone call.

She'd been excited, yet at the same time, worried. Worried Dan wouldn't be flexible and that she'd be forced to make a choice she didn't want to make.

While Dan had been supportive of Tess and her career, Tess had been his *wife*. She was just his employee. That's why her neck had been tied in knots. Even now just thinking about the decision she faced brought the weight back to her shoulders.

"Philippe from Chez Gladines had called," she said, then stopped. How much should she tell Dan? Was now really the best time? After all, she hadn't had a chance to consider the offer and decide what it was *she* wanted to do.

Obviously misunderstanding the uncertainty in her eyes, Dan leaned forward and took her hand. "Bad news?"

"Unexpected." Amy sighed. "Confusing."

"They were foolish to let you go." His fingers closed around hers. "I'm not going to make the same mistake."

"I don't think you understand." Amy began, "They didn't—"

"Because I know what a gem you are," Dan continued as if Amy hadn't spoken. "You're a wonderful woman. Smart. Fun. Not to mention incredibly sexy."

His eyes darkened. When he trailed a finger across the top of the sheet she forgot all about Philippe. When he cupped her chin and covered her mouth with his, she forgot everything but him. It was a gentle kiss, a sweet kiss, but Amy was in the mood for naughty, not nice. She grabbed Dan's head and deepened the kiss.

He responded immediately and she reveled in the moist heat and slow, penetrating slide of his tongue. He stroked long and slow, hot and deep, and she kissed him back the same way. Intense and uninhibited.

Just like last night, the room dipped and swayed. A purr of pleasure rumbled in her throat.

"I can't get enough of you," he whispered against her hair when she pulled away.

Amy caressed her palm along his cheek, skimmed her thumb

along his full bottom lip, her gaze riveted to his. "I feel the same way."

"You have to know how much I care for you."

Dan's voice grew husky. "There isn't anything I wouldn't do for you."

Amy's heart pounded. When she spoke, her voice seemed to come from far away. "What are you saying, Dan?"

"Last night gave me hope," he said. "Hope that you cared for me as more than just a friend."

Amy noticed he'd said *care,* not *love.* Then again, this was unchartered territory for both of them.

"I do care for you, Dan. Very much." Amy tried not to read too much into his words but she couldn't help but wonder if her dream of happily-ever-after was sitting on the bed with her. "Surely you know I'm not the type of woman to sleep with a guy unless I care for him."

A look of relief crossed his face. "I was hoping that was the case."

He shifted and reached into his pocket. When he pulled out a tiny velvet box and flipped it open, Amy gasped.

Without missing a beat, Dan slipped off the bed and dropped to one knee. "Amy Logan, would you do me the honor of becoming my wife?"

The room spun wildly. For a second Amy wondered if this was just another one of her vivid daydreams. She blinked once.

Dan was still there.

She blinked again.

He hadn't moved.

Her heart stuttered at the hope mixed with a healthy dose of uncertainty in his eyes.

Amy hesitated for a moment, wondering what had brought about this unexpected proposal. Had their recent closeness made him realize what her heart had known for so long?

She shifted her gaze to the antique diamond. Love welled up

from deep in her heart and spilled past her lips. "Yes, oh, yes, I'll marry you."

Dan smiled broadly and slipped the ring on her finger.

It fit perfectly.

Like it had been made for her.

It was a sign, Amy decided, a sign that she and Dan were meant to be together forever.

She couldn't take her eyes off the ring, *her* ring. She loved the way it sparkled in the light, loved the heavy filigreed work reminiscent of a bygone era. Most of all, she loved the man who'd given it to her.

"It was my grandmother's," he said hurriedly as if disturbed by her intense scrutiny. "If you don't like it—"

"I love it." Amy's fingers curved inward, protecting the ring. "I'll love it forever."

I'll love you forever.

His gaze searched hers. "You really mean that."

Amy's gaze dropped again to the stone then back to his face. Familiar. Known. Increasingly beloved. "Absolutely."

"It looks beautiful on you," he said. *"You* look beautiful."

Amy resisted the urge to laugh out loud. She couldn't remember the last time she'd been so happy. "This is a wonderful day."

"You're right." Dan's hand closed over hers. "I can't wait to tell Emma the news."

Amy giggled from sheer joy. "She'll be an adorable flower girl."

A look of surprise crossed Dan's face. "You want a big wedding?"

Amy hesitated. Like most women, from the time she'd been a little girl, she'd just assumed she'd have a wedding with all the trimmings. But she'd picked up on the reservation in Dan's tone and she wanted him to feel free to voice his preferences.

"I'm not sure," Amy said. "I guess I never thought much about it."

"Big or small, it's up to you." Dan brought her hand to his lips and nibbled on her fingers. "As long as it doesn't take too long to plan. I can't wait for you to be my wife."

An overwhelming feeling of love washed over Amy. "I can't wait for you to be my husband."

Dan smiled. "Want to go out and celebrate?"

"I'd love to celebrate," Amy said. "But we don't need to go out."

Her fingers reached for the buttons on his shirt. "We can do that just fine right here."

CHAPTER FIFTEEN

Amy took a sip of wine and stared at her hand. The light in the Italian restaurant might not be the best but the stone still glittered nicely. She lifted her gaze to find Dan staring with an indulgent smile.

"You have the most beautiful eyes," he said. "They sparkle when you look at the ring."

Heat rose up Amy's neck and she wasn't sure how to respond. He probably thought she was being ridiculous, going all gaga over a diamond. It wasn't only the ring, it was the sentiment behind it that made her all soft and mushy inside.

"I didn't mean to embarrass you." Dan reached across the table and took her hand. "I'm happy you're so excited. I'm excited, too. We're going to have a great marriage."

The bustle of the popular eatery faded and Amy found herself drowning in the deep blue of Dan's eyes. Of course, they would have a great marriage. With love as its foundation...

Her thoughts stilled. When they'd made love, when he'd proposed, when they'd hopped into bed again to celebrate, not one 'I love you" had crossed his lips. Amy knew that for a fact since she'd been waiting for him to seal their union with the words. Still, how could they have connected so profoundly in bed if love wasn't at the foundation of their relationship?

"Penny for your thoughts." His thumb caressed the top of her hand.

Guilt coursed through her. This was supposed to be a celebration and here she was ruining it by worrying about who was going to say those three little words first.

"Tell me," Dan said.

Amy wasn't about to demand he declare his feelings. There *was* still some unfinished business to discuss.

"I was just thinking about my conversation with Philippe."

When Amy had spoken with Philippe, she'd feared she'd have to choose between the job and her life with Dan and Emma. Now, she thought happily, she could have it all.

Dan released her hand and took a sip of wine. "Don't give him a second thought. It's his loss."

"You don't understand." Amy couldn't keep the note of pride from her voice. "Philippe offered me a full-time position. My desserts have been a big hit and he asked me to be in charge of all desserts."

"Wow." Dan raked a hand through his hair and sat back, appearing more stunned than pleased by the news. "I don't know what to say."

"How about 'congratulations'?" Disappointment at his lack of enthusiasm made her voice sharper than she'd intended. "Philippe could have offered this position to a dozen other chefs."

"I'm sorry. Congratulations." His tone was sincere and apologetic and her anger eased. "I'm not surprised they want you. You're a great chef."

Amy's heart warmed at the praise and she felt her irritation melt away. "Thank you, Dan."

He forked a piece of ravioli and brought it to his mouth. "What did he say when you told him you couldn't do it?"

Amy nearly choked on her orzo. She took a sip of water and

straightened in her seat, taking a moment to compose herself before responding.

"You don't want me to take it?" Disappointment ran thick and heavy through her voice. Right or wrong, not having him share in the joy took some of the luster off the offer.

"Are you really considering it?"

She ignored the shock and disbelief in his voice and nodded.

Dan's eyes grew shuttered. "You need to do what's best for you."

"No." Amy leaned forward and rested her forearms on the table. "This isn't just about me anymore. When you get married, the other person's happiness should be as important as your own. You assumed I wouldn't take the job. I need to know what your reservations are."

Dan wiped the corners of his mouth with the tip of his linen napkin, his expression still guarded. "Call me selfish but I like having you around. Since Emma is in school all day, I know you've had more free time. After we're married, I was hoping we could eventually start working on giving Emma a couple of brothers or sisters—"

He stopped and Amy realized she must look as startled as she felt. "Unless you don't want children. We've never discussed it but I know how much you like kids. I just assumed you'd want a baby or two..."

Amy's breath caught in her throat. Dan wanted her to have his baby. Her hand moved to her flat belly. What would it be like, Amy wondered, to have Dan's baby? Of course, last night he'd taken precautions to ensure that wouldn't happen, but she couldn't imagine anything more wonderful than to have a child grow out of the love they shared.

He really *did* love her. A lump rose in Amy's throat. Tears filled her eyes.

"Hey." He grabbed her hand. "If you don't want—"

"I'd love to have a baby." Her voice trembled with emotion. "Actually, I want lots of babies. A whole houseful."

"Good," he said and she could hear the relief in his voice. "That's settled."

In her happy fog, it took a second for Amy to realize that not only had she agreed to have a baby, somehow she'd agreed to give up her career. A momentary pang hit her. Even if she got pregnant right away, it'd be almost a year until a baby came. During that time she could get some great experience at Chez Gladines. Not to mention contacts that could be invaluable if she chose to continue with her own catering business.

"Ready to go home and plan a wedding?" Dan's deep voice broke through her fog. "I'm thinking something small, but nice, where Emma could play a part."

Amy liked the thought of Emma being involved.

"We can pick up the license tomorrow and get married next week. Unless," he added, almost as an afterthought, "you want a big wedding?"

The way he said the words made it clear that wouldn't be his preference. While part of her wanted a big wedding with the long white dress, the sensible side said she was being foolish. Other than Aunt Verna she had no family and only a handful of friends.

"Not big." Amy hesitated. "I do want to get married in a church and have a small reception."

"That shouldn't be too difficult to arrange."

Amy's head spun, barely able to fathom that in one week she could be Dan's *wife*.

"Would you two care for dessert?" The waiter stood tableside, pad in hand and pencil poised.

Amy glanced at Dan. "I don't care for any."

"None for me, either," Dan said. "I'll wait until we get home."

Amy waited until the waiter left before casting a curious glance at Dan. "The chocolate cake is all gone. You ate the last of it yesterday."

"That wasn't the dessert I was thinking of." His gaze dropped to her lips, then downward to her breasts before returning to her eyes.

The rush of hunger that surged through Amy surprised her with its intensity. They'd made love several times during the night and again this morning. Instead of being satiated, her desire for him only seemed to grow.

"I'm hungry, too," Amy said. "Mind if I join you?"

Dan's smile widened and a devilish glint filled his eyes. "I wouldn't have it any other way."

The next morning, they made love one more time knowing it would be the last time until after the wedding. Once Emma returned from her friend's house, Dan would stay in his room and Amy would stay in hers.

After they dressed, Amy started toward the door, already planning what she was going to make for lunch, when Dan grabbed her hand.

"Not so fast," he said with a smile. "How about we walk down to Bagels and Jam? You can get one of those chocolate chip scones you like so much and I can sit and admire your beauty under the fluorescent lights."

Amy laughed at the absurd compliment, but she didn't refute the words because when she was with Dan she *felt* beautiful.

"It'll be like a date," she said lightly.

His hand cupped her cheek and his lips met hers for a warm, sweet kiss. "A date with my almost-wife."

Amy flushed with pleasure. He threw that word around as if he loved the sound of it as much as she did. Today, they'd start letting people know. She'd call Aunt Verna. Dan would call his mother and Tess's parents. Then it would be official.

As they left the house and strolled down the leaf-strewn

sidewalk, contentment wrapped itself around Amy like a favorite coat. The temperature hovered in the mid-forties and the sun shone warm against her face. Even the breeze held some warmth.

Walking down the street with her hand nestled in Dan's, happiness welled inside her. Amy wanted to whistle. If she'd been a better singer she might have burst into song.

My cup runneth over.

She'd never truly understood those words before now. Impulsively Amy stopped and pulled Dan to her. She wrapped her arms around him and pressed a long, lingering kiss against his lips.

"Wow," he said, a broad grin splitting his face. "What was that for?"

"I'm so happy," Amy said.

Dan trailed a finger down her cheek. "I feel the same way."

He took her hand and they continued down the street.

"You know what's crazy?" Amy said, after they'd gone another block. She didn't wait for an answer since the question was strictly rhetorical. "When people used to talk about finding their soul mate, I thought it was corny. Now I understand. That's exactly how I feel about you."

Dan's fingers tightened around hers but he didn't have a chance to speak because the bagel shop loomed and he gallantly stepped forward to open the door for a woman in front of them.

The woman, a statuesque brunette with sprinkles of gray in her hair, looked back. Instead of moving through the doorway, she paused. Her lips curved up into a broad smile.

"Why, Dan Major, what a surprise." The woman shot him an exaggerated wink. "We're going to have to stop meeting like this."

Beside her, Amy felt Dan stiffen but his smile was warm. "How nice to see you again."

Amy had met most of Dan's friends but this woman wasn't the least bit familiar. She stood beside Dan, patiently waiting for an introduction. While Dan normally had excellent manners, he made no attempt to introduce her. It suddenly hit Amy that he must have forgotten the woman's name.

"Hello," Amy said pleasantly, holding out her hand. "I'm Amy Logan."

"I'm sorry." Dan quickly recovered. "Amy, this is Angela Bartgate. She used to be a neighbor."

"Pleased to meet you, Amy." Angela took Amy's outstretched hand and shook it, her smile open and friendly.

A gust of wind blew Amy's hair into her face. When Amy reached up with her free hand to push the wayward strands back, Angela gasped.

'What a stunning ring," the woman said.

Amy proudly held out her hand. The stone shot sparks of color in the sunlight. "It originally belonged to Dan's grandmother."

"It's lovely." Angela's gaze shifted from Amy to Dan before returning to Amy. "I must say this is quite a surprise. Dan and I ran into each other yesterday morning and he didn't say a word about being engaged."

Amy laughed. "That's because he hadn't popped the question yet."

"Soon you'll be newlyweds." Angela's eyes softened. "I remember when my husband and I were first married..."

Angela began to reminisce and somehow—Amy wasn't quite sure how—she and Dan found themselves sitting with Angela.

Normally quite social, Dan seemed unusually quiet. Or maybe it was because Angela kept asking questions and Amy kept answering. By the time Amy finished her scone, she figured Angela probably knew as much about her as her closest friends.

Every so often Dan would throw out a comment, some anecdote about something they'd shared and Amy had to resist the urge to pinch herself to make sure this was real.

Dan glanced at his watch. "We're going to have to get going. I told Ted we'd pick up Emma."

He'd barely finished speaking when his phone rang. Dan pulled it from his pocket and glanced at the readout.

"I need to take this." He rose to his feet. "If you'll excuse me..."

Dan moved to the far end of the shop where there were more empty tables and less chatter. Amy's eyes weren't the only ones that followed him. She caught several women staring. Women always noticed Dan.

Yet, he'd chosen her. Amy still couldn't believe it. He could have had almost any woman.

"You love him."

Amy pulled her thoughts back and looked up to find Angela's gaze on her. She thought about denying it, but decided she was being ridiculous. Dan was her fiancé. Love was supposed to be part of the equation.

"I do love him," Amy said. "It took me a while to realize it but I think I've loved him for a long time."

A thoughtful look crossed Angela's face. "He loves you, too."

"What makes you so sure?" Amy's lighthearted tone was at odds with her rapidly beating heart. Somehow she even managed to throw in a little laugh. "Other than this ring on my finger, of course."

"The way he looks at you," Angela said. "My husband, Tom, used to look at me that same way."

A warm rush of pleasure washed over Amy, quieting her fears.

Angela shook her head. "I can't believe how much that man had me fooled."

"Your husband?"

"No, your fiancé," Angela said. "Yesterday when we talked Dan had me actually believing his next marriage would be based on practicality, not love. Now he shows up madly in love and engaged."

Amy swallowed hard past the sudden lump in her throat. *Practicality?* Had Dan just been playing a part for Angela? Or was that how he truly felt?

Angela took both of Amy's hands in hers. "I'm so very, very happy for you both."

Amy's only response was a wan smile.

Very, very happy?

That's the way she should feel. Instead, Amy had never felt worse.

CHAPTER SIXTEEN

When Dan had returned from his phone call and told Amy that Jake was coming over, she turned quiet and solemn. As they walked home, she scarcely spoke. He wondered if she was upset that he hadn't talked much around Angela. The truth of the matter was he felt awkward after his previous conversation with the woman. Not to mention he didn't want to give Angela a chance to bring up what they'd discussed.

Or she could be upset because he'd left her to talk to Jake. She'd seemed in good spirits up to that point.

He took her hand, surprised to find her fingers ice cold. "I didn't mean for us to get stuck spending all that time with Angela."

"That's okay," Amy said, not looking at him. "She's a nice woman."

A sense of unease crept up Dan's spine. Something wasn't right but he couldn't put his finger on what.

"Jake won't stay long," Dan said. He'd tried to tell his friend today wasn't good, but as usual Jake didn't listen. "He has a problem with a project he's working on that supposedly needs immediate resolution."

"I've been thinking," Amy said slowly, keeping her gaze focused straight ahead. "It might be better if we didn't tell any more people about the engagement. Not just yet."

"Why would we want to do that?" he asked slowly. Now that Amy had agreed to marry him, he didn't want her to change her mind.

Amy lifted a shoulder in a shrug.

"Everything has moved along pretty fast," Amy said, sounding incredibly weary. "It might be good to slow things down a bit."

Red flags popped up in Dan's head. He didn't want to read too much into what she was saying. Still, between her body language and her words, he had the definite impression she was getting cold feet

"Is it—" he took a deep breath and plunged ahead "—that you're not sure you want to marry me?"

He cast a sideways glance, surprised to discover Amy wasn't at his side. He spun on his heel and found her standing in the middle of the sidewalk.

"This isn't about me." Amy's voice was so low he could barely hear her. "It's about you."

"Me?" Dan's heart beat like a hammer in his' chest. "What about me?"

"Angela said when you two talked before she'd gotten the impression if you did marry again it would be because of practicality, not love." Even though the day was warm, Amy crossed her arms over her chest as if she were cold. "Is that why you're marrying me, Dan? Because I'm quick and convenient?"

Ah, now he understood.

Amy did a good job keeping the pain from her voice but Dan knew her too well to be fooled. Angela's words had hurt her. Dan clenched his jaw. Next time he saw the woman he'd let her know what he thought of her meddling.

"For your information Angela brought up the topic of marrying for companionship, not love," Dan said. "I already *have* friends and companions. I don't need to marry to have that."

Amy's gaze searched his. Whatever she saw there must have satisfied her because she smiled and didn't object when he took her hand.

As they walked home Dan couldn't help but wonder if she'd noticed he hadn't fully answered her question.

He still hadn't said he loved her.

Amy listened to Emma's chatter in the car with half an ear. When Jake had arrived, Amy had volunteered to pick up Emma. She'd planned to walk to the Martins's house knowing that would give her even more time alone, more time to think. The wind had picked up and the air had taken on a decided chill.

When Amy had pulled into the Martins's driveway she'd taken off the ring before getting out of the car. While Dan's comments on their walk home had partially allayed her fears, she hadn't wanted to get the girl's hopes up. Not until she was absolutely sure Dan was marrying her out of love, not practicality.

She loved Emma too much to cause her pain.

But Dan loves Emma, too.

Not to mention, he wants us to start a family. A man wouldn't do that with someone he didn't love, someone he considered only a companion.

"Are you going to read to me tonight, Amy?" Emma asked.

Amy blinked and shifted her gaze to Emma. "I am. How far did you get last night?"

The *Humphrey* books were above Emma's reading level but perfect for reading to her. On Thursday night they'd finished the first book in the series and Emma had taken the second, *Friendship According to Humphrey,* with her to her friend's house.

A look of disappointment crossed Emma's face. "Nina's mother didn't have time."

It didn't surprise Amy. Abigail Martin had been one of Tess's closest friends. She was very nice, just not very child oriented.

"Well, I must say that's good news," Amy said.

Emma looked quizzical.

Amy shot her a wink. "I won't need to catch up on what I missed."

The giggle that escaped from Emma's lips made Amy smile. Her heart swelled with love. If she and Dan did marry, she'd not only be Dan's wife, she'd be Emma's mother. Stepmother, she corrected herself. But she didn't feel like a step-anything. She couldn't love Emma more if the little girl was her own.

For a second Amy was tempted to open her purse, pull out the ring and put it on...

"Amy." Emma squirmed in her seat. "Can you unlock the door? Rehn is on her porch and I want to say hi."

Amy slowed the car as they neared the house. Rehn, the little girl who lived next door, was outside helping her mother put up holiday decorations. Pulling to a stop into the driveway, Amy unlocked the car door.

"Put up your hood." Amy's tone brooked no argument. "I want you in the house in five minutes. That'll give you plenty of time to say hello. Understand?"

Emma nodded, opened the car door and slid out.

Amy waved to Rehn and her mother before pulling into the garage. Rehn's mother, Margaret, had a life Amy envied. A rewarding career. Three beautiful children. *And* a loving husband.

Yes, Margaret had it all. Just like Amy would have if she married Dan.

Amy pulled the ring from her purse and put it on.

She'd been foolish to doubt Dan. Her life was on the upswing and the way she looked at it, it could only get better.

Dan glanced at the clock on the wall and wondered when Jake was going to leave. Amy and Emma should be back any minute and he wanted his friend gone.

Instead of getting up to leave, Jake leaned back in his chair as if he had all the time in the world. "So how *is* our favorite nanny? Are we going to be hearing wedding bells soon?"

Dan didn't really want to discuss his engagement with Jake but he certainly didn't want him hearing it from someone else and jumping to all the wrong conclusions.

"As a matter of fact, yes," Dan said after a long pause. "I asked Amy to marry me last night."

Amy paused in the hallway just outside the dining room. She'd seen Jake's car in the driveway and planned to slip up the back-stairs but when she heard her name, she couldn't help herself from eavesdropping. She'd always had a curious streak and she couldn't wait to hear what Dan would say. Would he tell Jake he loved her?

Amy held her breath.

"Did she accept?" Jake asked.

"She did."

Amy smiled at the satisfaction in Dan's voice.

"Way to go, buddy," Jake said. "I didn't think you'd pull it off."

Amy pulled her brows together. Pull what off?

"When you said you were going to make her fall in love with you, I wasn't sure you could do it," Jake continued. "You were determined."

"Jake—" Dan began.

"'Course you had a lot riding on this," Jake said. "Those in-laws of yours won't have a snowball's chance in hell of getting

Emma now if anything happens to you. Especially if you have Amy adopt her."

Amy's heart pounded. Her knees went weak. She placed a hand against the wall to steady herself. The proposal had all been part of a plan? A scheme?

"It's not about that—" Dan said.

"'Course not," Jake interrupted with a sardonic laugh. "Like I told you before, for the price of a ring and marriage license you get a nanny, a housekeeper and someone to warm your bed. I'm happy you finally listened. Say, what's she like in the sack? Any good?"

Dan murmured something Amy couldn't hear. It didn't matter. She'd heard enough. Amy choked back a sob, remembering Angela's words about Dan's motives for marriage. The woman had been right the first time.

Dan's proposal didn't have a thing to do with love.

Making it through the rest of the day took every ounce of Amy's strength. If this just involved her and Dan, she'd have packed her bags, thrown the ring in his face and walked out without looking back. Because of Emma, Amy pretended she hadn't overheard Dan's conversation with Jake.

She plastered a smile on her face, made dinner and ignored Dan's teasing comments and flirtatious looks. When it came time for Emma's bedtime, she asked Dan if she could put Emma to bed herself. By the pleased look in his eye, she knew he thought she was planning to discuss their engagement with the little girl. Amy saw no reason to correct him.

Emma begged her to read an extra chapter and instead of just one, Amy read three. She savored every moment knowing this was the last time she and Emma would share a bedtime story.

As she read, Amy's eyes filled with tears. When Emma

noticed, Amy blamed it on the story. Finally, Amy closed the book. She could no longer delay the inevitable. She shut her eyes for a moment and prayed for the right words. Words that would convey to Emma how much she was loved. Words that would help the child to understand that none of this was her fault.

"Emma." Amy cleared her throat and clutched her hands together to still their trembling. She did her best to inject some excitement into her voice. "I got some fabulous news today."

Emma tilted her head. Despite the late hour her eyes were bright and inquisitive. "You did?"

"Mmm-hmm." Amy forced a smile to her face. "The restaurant offered me a full-time position."

"That's good," Emma said. "Right?"

"Very good." The tightness in Amy's chest made it difficult to speak. She leaned forward, brushing Emma's silky hair back from her sweet face. "Unfortunately it's going to take a lot of my time."

"I'll help," Emma said. "I'm a good helper."

"Yes, you are." Amy drew a ragged breath. This wasn't going at all the way she hoped. She tried a different tactic. "You remember my aunt Verna?"

Emma nodded. "She gave me your stinky."

Startled, Amy sat back. "Stinky?"

"It goes down the steps."

"Oh, you mean *Slinky.*" Her aunt had won the girl over with that gift.

"Anyway." Amy took a deep breath. "Aunt Verna has a new house and she wants me to live with her."

Emma's tiny brow furrowed. "But you live here."

At that moment, Amy would have given anything to go back to the way it used to be—when Dan was only her employer and not her lover, when life was simple and uncomplicated. Or did everything happen to push her in a direction she wouldn't have gone otherwise?

"My aunt needs me." Amy took Emma's hand. "I'll be around so much you won't even have a chance to miss me."

Tears welled up in Emma's blue eyes. "I don't want you to leave."

Amy swallowed past the lump in her throat. "We'll see each other all the time. I promise."

"I love you." Emma's voice trembled.

"I love you, too, princess." Amy brushed her tears away with the back of her hand. "That will never change."

"Promise?"

Amy wanted to sob at the trust in the little girl's eyes.

"I promise. I'll always be in your heart." Amy placed her hand against her chest. "You'll always be in mine."

She bent over and kissed the little girl's forehead, her own tears mingling with Emma's. She sat at the bedside for the longest time, stroking the child's hair and murmuring words of reassurance until Emma drifted off to sleep.

If there was a way she could stay and retain her dignity, Amy would do it for the sake of Emma. The little girl deserved a better role model than a woman who'd let a man use her.

Amy deserved better, too. That's why, after she told Dan just what she thought of him and his deception, she was walking out the door.

Dan leaned back in his favorite chair, his fingers laced behind his head. He hoped he'd read all the signs correctly and that Amy was upstairs now telling Emma about the engagement.

While he'd thought they'd tell Emma together, when Amy said she wanted to tuck in Emma alone, he didn't protest. Amy had always been very sensitive to Emma's feelings, and if *she* felt broaching the subject one-on-one was best, he'd defer to her judgment.

He'd never have been able to do that with Tess. Children to her were mysterious creatures. She'd loved Emma to death but she'd never understood Emma's sensitive nature. Amy, on the other hand, knew just how to handle the little girl, probably because she and Emma were so much alike.

Footsteps sounded on the stairs and Dan's pulse quickened. *Let the celebration begin.* He knew Amy wouldn't sleep with him, not with Emma in the house. But he might be able to steal a kiss or two...

The door to the parlor opened and Dan stood, a welcoming smile already on his lips. His smile faded at Amy's tear-streaked face. It was obvious by the bleak look in Amy's eyes that Emma hadn't taken the news well.

Dan hurried across the room, knowing whatever objections Emma had could be easily dealt with. The last thing he wanted was for Amy to be discouraged.

"She'll come around." Dan reached for Amy, surprised when she jerked away. For Amy to be this upset, Emma must have pitched an all-out fit. "I'll talk to her."

"I think you better," Amy said, her voice cool and measured. "After we talk."

Dan wanted to pull her into his arms and reassure her that this would all work out, but her stiff body posture and crossed arms clearly said "hands off."

"I'm moving out," Amy said. "I know an older woman who is between assignments who'll be happy to help you out while you look for someone permanent."

Dan's overstressed mind fought to make sense of what she was saying.

"Move out?" He pulled his brows together in puzzlement. "You mean until after the wedding?"

"There's not going to be a wedding," Amy said flatly.

Now she was talking crazy. Emma loved Amy. Whatever

Emma had said to upset Amy, she couldn't have meant. "What did Emma say?"

"This doesn't have anything to do with her." Amy's voice rose. "It's about you and why you want to marry me."

Dan's blood turned to ice.

She'd overheard his conversation with Jake. That had to be the explanation. Dan tried to remember what Jake had said—and what he'd said—but, at the moment, his rioting emotions seemed to be short-circuiting his brain.

"I know about Emma's grandparents and your fear that if anything happened to you they might get custody," she said when he remained silent.

"That wasn't why I asked you to marry me." The words tumbled from his lips. "I admit that may have started me thinking about marriage, but that isn't why I asked you."

She opened her mouth, then shut it, the momentary indecision giving him hope. He gestured to the sofa. "Why don't we sit down and talk?"

Amy didn't even glance in the sofa's direction. "I have one question."

"Anything." He found himself encouraged by the continuing dialogue. If he could just keep her here and talking, he knew they could work things out.

"Do you love me, Dan?" Amy's gaze met his. "Not as a friend, but the way a man should love a woman he wants to marry."

Dan paused and tried to convince himself that he could say yes and have it not be a lie. He did care for Amy and compared to some of his friends, his feelings went far beyond what they appeared to feel for their wives.

Dan opened his mouth but Amy spoke first. "The way you loved Tess."

Everything in Dan went cold. Why did she have to bring up Tess? What he'd felt for his wife had been a once-in-a-lifetime thing.

"Amy, I—" Dan reached out to her, then let his hand drop. "You know how I felt about Tess."

A sad little smile touched Amy's lips. "I want that, too. I want someone who's crazy about me. Someone who can't live without me."

Her lips began to tremble. Swallowing a sob, Amy turned on her heel and ran down the hall.

"Don't go. Please." Dan hurried after her, his heart in his throat. His panic increased when he saw her bags sitting on the kitchen floor. "We can make this work."

"We could." Amy turned toward him, her eyes reflecting her pain. "But we're not. I'm not going to spend my life being second best to a dead woman."

"You're not—" He stopped himself.

"I have dreams, too," Amy said. "Things that are important to me."

"What are you talking about?"

"The job at Chez Gladines." Amy lifted her chin. "Did you even once stop to ask me what I wanted to do, what I thought would be best?"

The accusatory tone took Dan by surprise. His temper surged.

"I thought getting married was what you wanted." Hurt mingled with his anger. "I thought you liked taking care of our home and being with me. You're just like Tess. Not content to be a wife and mother. Always wanting more."

The words came from his lips, but Dan couldn't believe he'd said them. Couldn't believe he'd *thought* them.

"I do want more." Amy met his gaze. "I want your love. I want your support. I don't have either. That's why the engagement's off."

CHAPTER SEVENTEEN

Amy hadn't raised her voice above a normal conversational level but tension hung thick in the air. Though she'd done a good job of keeping her composure, Amy was a quivering mass of nerves inside.

She couldn't imagine walking out of the house that had been her home for the past three years. She couldn't imagine leaving Emma. She couldn't imagine leaving Dan. Or at least the Dan she thought she loved. She couldn't stay now. Her heart hardened against the pain. She'd respected Dan. She'd trusted him. It only made his betrayal the harder to bear.

"We can work this out." Dan shoved his hands in his pockets and rocked back on his heels.

Amy sighed. "How, Dan? Are you going to make yourself love me?"

After what he'd done, after what he'd left unsaid, pulling the ring off her finger and handing it to him should have been easy. Still, she hesitated.

"I was afraid if anything happened to me, Tess's parents would fight for custody." A hint of desperation filled Dan's voice. "You know what they're like."

"I thought I was in your will as her guardian?"

"You are," Dan said. "But Gwen made it clear that she'd never let a nonrelative raise Emma."

"I have to hand it to you. Your plan almost worked." Slipping off the ring, Amy held it out to him. "Take it."

"I don't want it." His gaze never left her face. "I gave it to you."

Amy glanced at the clock on the kitchen wall. Steven should be here any minute to pick her up. Not that she was rushing because of that. If she thought the wall between them could be scaled by simply talking, she'd stay all night.

Dan didn't love her. There was nothing to discuss.

Amy placed the ring on the counter, then turned to Dan. "I left Aunt Verna's address, as well as the name of the woman I mentioned, on the dresser in my room. You can send my last paycheck to Verna's. I'll be staying with her until I find a place of my own."

Before the last of the words had left her mouth, Dan was beside her, wrapping his arms around her, pulling her close. For a second Amy just stood there, absorbing the warmth from his body, breathing in the familiar spicy scent of his cologne, feeling his strength.

"I don't want you to leave." Dan whispered against her hair. "I care about you so much. Can't we build on that?"

A horn honked, but when Amy tried to slip from Dan's embrace, his arms remained tightly locked around her.

"It's too late," Amy said, her voice hardly above a whisper. "You know as well as I do that we can't go back to the way it was before."

Dan stood motionless, his heart beating a rapid rhythm against her. "What about Emma?"

Amy hesitated. A clean break might be the easiest for her but she knew that wouldn't be the best for Emma.

"I'd like to continue to be a part of her life," Amy said, the words coming out in a rush. "She never knew things had gotten...more intense between you and me, so it shouldn't be awkward. That is, if you don't mind."

"I'd like that." Dan cleared his throat. "She's going to miss you."

He loosened his hold and Amy stepped back.

"My continuing to live here would never work."

A horn sounded again and Dan swore. "Who is making all that noise?"

"Steven."

Dan's gaze narrowed.

"I called him." Amy lifted her chin. "He's giving me a ride to my aunt's house."

She'd tried to reach Verna, but the call had gone straight to the recorder. Amy didn't want to spend another night under Dan's roof. If Verna wasn't home when she got there, she'd have Steven drop her at a motel.

"You didn't need to call him." A tiny muscle jumped in Dan's jaw. "You have the Volvo."

"You bought the car for Emma's nanny," Amy pointed out "You'll need it for the woman who takes my place."

Dan's gaze met hers. "No one will ever take your place."

Amy didn't bother answering. Dan may not want to hire another nanny but he would. With his work commitments he couldn't take care of Emma by himself. He'd do what he had to do.

She'd do the same. By walking out the door.

As they sat at the stoplight just down the street from Dan's house, Amy sensed Steven's gaze on her. Instead of looking in his direction, she kept her head back and her eyes half shut.

She knew it was rude but she didn't feel much like talking. Her emotions were too raw, too close to the surface.

When she'd called and asked Steven for a ride he'd said yes without asking any questions. She'd known he was curious, but thankfully too polite to probe. Unfortunately, Dan standing in the doorway watching them load the bags in the car appeared to have pushed his curiosity to the breaking point.

"What happened?" Steven asked. "What made you finally decide to move out?"

Heaving a resigned sigh Amy opened her eyes and turned to face Steven. She owed him some sort of explanation. After all, he'd just gotten back into town, yet he'd dropped everything to pick her up.

"I have a new job." Amy forced a smile and tried to drum up her earlier enthusiasm. "Chez Gladines wants me full-time."

A startled look crossed Steven's face and she could tell it wasn't the answer he'd expected. Still, he quickly rallied, his lips curving up into a broad smile. "Congratulations. That's fabulous news."

Amy shifted her gaze, finding his joyousness almost painful. She picked at a loose thread on her coat. "Yes, I guess it is."

His brows drew together in puzzlement. "You don't seem excited."

"It's a lot of responsibility," Amy said. "I'll be in charge of all the desserts, not just pastries."

She'd never doubted herself before but the experience with Dan had left her feeling unsettled.

"You'll do a great job." As if he could read her mind, Steven reached over and gave her hand a squeeze. "I knew it was just a matter of time. Once they got a taste of your talent, how could they not want more?"

His generous words acted as a soothing balm on her wounded spirit. Steven was such a great guy. He had so much to offer a woman. Life would be so much easier if only she could love him instead of Dan. Amy sighed.

"You're the best," Amy said. "Anyone ever tell you that?"

"Every day," Steven said, shooting her a wink before his gaze turned speculative. "How did Dan take the news?"

"Not well." It was an understatement but Amy didn't feel like elaborating.

"Did he give you an ultimatum?" Steven probed. "Is that why you moved out in the middle of the night?"

Amy shrugged. "You know Dan. Everything has to be his way."

It wasn't completely true or for that matter, particularly fair. If Amy were feeling generous, she'd correct the mistaken impression. At the moment she wasn't feeling kind *or* generous.

"It must have been hard to realize your dreams mattered so little," Steven mused. "I know how much you like him."

Amy stared out the passenger window into the inky darkness. Tonight she'd been forced to face facts. To toss aside her rose-colored glasses and see Dan for who he was and not how she wished he could be.

A wave of sadness washed over Amy. The truth was Dan didn't love her. Heck, he probably didn't even like her all that much. Everything he'd done, everything he'd said, had been a means to an end.

Her heart hardened.

"I used to like Dan." Amy closed her eyes and leaned back against the seat. "Not anymore."

"Daddy, is Amy coming home today?"

Dan's hand paused on the can of green beans. Pain stabbed him and the loneliness he'd fought to contain returned full force. He turned to find Emma staring at him over the top of the grocery cart.

"No." He kept his tone matter-of-fact. "Not today."

It had been four long weeks since Amy had moved out and

the house seemed empty without her. Every day, Emma asked if Amy was coming home. At first, the question prompted long discussions. He'd emphasize that Amy still loved her and would be seeing her regularly. She just kept asking. After a while Dan just started saying no, not today.

Usually Emma went on to talk about Amy. Today, Dan wasn't in the mood to listen to his daughter go on and on about how wonderful Amy was.

The last time she'd stopped over to take Emma to the children's museum, she'd *looked* wonderful. Her hair had been layered, giving it a stylish, windblown appearance. The coat she'd been wearing had been one of those fur-trimmed ones that was all the rage.

To his critical eye she'd looked thinner and he wondered if she'd been eating properly. Or maybe she'd been sick. There'd been no time to ask because she'd whisked Emma out of the house without giving him a chance to say much more than hello and goodbye.

"...and Steven."

He blinked, the can of green beans still in his hand. "What did you say?"

"I climbed on the fire engine at the children's museum," Emma said. "Then Amy and Steven got me ice cream."

Dan dropped the can into the cart and counted to ten. He'd agreed to Amy spending time with Emma but that didn't include her boyfriend. "I didn't know Steven went with you to the children's museum."

"He didn't," Emma stood on her tiptoes and peered into the cart. She wrinkled her nose. "Green beans. Yuck."

"They're good for you," Dan said absently. "What do you mean Steven didn't come with you? I thought you said you all had ice cream."

"After the museum, me and Amy went to the mall." Emma's

eyes brightened. "I like the mall. Will you take me there some-time, Daddy?"

"Sure," Dan said. "So you met Steven at the mall?"

He didn't know why he was pushing so hard for details. After all, as long as Steven hadn't deliberately been part of the outing, it wasn't any of his concern.

"He was at the store that had all the pretty jewelry," Emma said. "Buying Christmas presents."

Emma twirled in the aisle. "I want lots and lots of pretty presents."

Dan tuned her out. He'd already heard too much. Steven had been looking at jewelry. Buying presents. Probably picking out *Amy's* Christmas gift.

Steven was a successful, eligible bachelor who seemed genuinely interested in Amy. Dan knew he should be happy for her. All he felt was jealous. He wanted to be the one buying her ice cream on a Sunday afternoon. He wanted to be sitting across the supper table from her, talking about the day and laughing with her at Emma's knock-knock jokes. At night he wanted to be the one in her bed. If anyone was buying her jewelry, Dan wanted it to be him.

His jaw tightened.

"Steven's taking Amy to a party Wednesday night, so she can't come see me." Emma's smile turned to a pout. "It's not fair. Wednesday night is *my* night."

Shortly after Amy moved out, they'd set up a visitation sched-ule. She took Emma every Wednesday night and every Sunday. This would be the first time she'd canceled.

Not many women would have been so diligent. Most of the ones he knew put career and their various social obligations before children. Tess, he'd finally come to realize, had been no exception.

When Dan had married Tess, he hadn't thought much about the kind of wife and mother she'd be. All he knew was that they were happy and in love. As time went on, he found himself wishing she didn't see the need to be so involved in everything. He'd gotten tired of eating out every night and always being on the run.

He'd hoped she'd slow down after Emma was born, but if anything, the pace only picked up. Maybe it was a good thing Amy had backed out of their engagement. When she'd talked about working fulltime at Chez Gladines it was as if she'd taken a knife to the heart. The last thing he wanted was to come in a distant second to her career. Like he had with Tess.

Still, Dan missed Amy. Marjorie, the woman who Amy had recommended, kept the house clean and took good care of Emma. But without Amy, the house no longer felt like a home.

"I want to go to the party with Steven and Amy." Emma clasped her hands together. "Can I, Daddy? Can I go?"

Dan only wished he could grant Emma's wish. He'd love to send his daughter along as a chaperone. But he knew Amy needed to get on with her life, just as he did. He threw a box of cereal into the cart and shook his head, unruffled by Emma's pleading expression.

"The only place we're going is home." He tapped her on the nose. "Grandpa Phil and Grandma Gwen are coming tonight and they're bringing your presents."

Emma gave an excited squeal and Dan smiled. At least one of them was happy about the visit. He couldn't complain because he was the one who'd invited them.

In preparation for tonight, he'd made a quick trip to his attorney's office and had gotten the information he'd needed, information he should have gotten a long time ago. After dinner, he'd send Emma up to her room to play with her toys. Then he would have a talk with Gwen and Phil. A long overdue talk.

CHAPTER EIGHTEEN

Dan glanced around the grand ballroom of the Michigan Avenue hotel, which had been transformed into a Winter Wonderland. Fake snow and ice sculptures, red and white roses as well as the more traditional poinsettias and garlands of greenery were everywhere. The laughter of the festive holiday crowd filled the air.

With a resigned sigh, Dan snagged a glass of champagne from a passing waiter. He'd planned to spend the night playing board games with Emma, but at the last minute one of the other partners couldn't attend the mayor's Christmas Gala, and Dan had been roped into going.

Christmas.

The big day was less than a week away and Dan hadn't bought a single gift or even put up the tree. Christmas had always been his favorite holiday but this year he hadn't been able to summon up much enthusiasm.

The season was off to a great start. Amy had moved out. Then, Phil and Gwen had left in a huff barely twenty-four hours after they'd arrived. To top it off, his mother and stepfather had decided at the last minute to spend the holidays in Texas with his aunt.

This year it would be just him and Emma. The fact that his mother and Hal wouldn't be spending the holidays with them didn't bother him. Not as much as the knowledge that, for the first time in three years, Amy wouldn't be at his side. He shoved the disturbing thought aside.

Mistletoe hung at discreet locations throughout the room. Dan felt a tap on his shoulder and realized with horror that he was standing under one of the sprigs. One of the wives of a prominent city official loved to kiss men she found standing under the mistletoe and for a second Dan feared he'd been caught.

He turned and breathed a sigh of relief. "Bree. What a pleasant surprise."

Dressed in a clingy copper-colored dress with a front that was cut almost as low as the back, Bree looked more like a sexy chorus girl than a respected tax attorney.

"Merry Christmas, Dan." Bree put her hands on his shoulders and brushed a friendly kiss across his lips. She took a step back and gazed up at him, as if waiting for his reaction.

"Merry Christmas to you, too." Dan glanced around. "Who'd you come with?"

"I'm alone." Her lips pulled together in a cute little pout. "Poor little Bree, doesn't have a date."

"If it makes you feel better, I'm in the same boat." Dan's lips lifted In a rueful smile. "This was Harry's year to come but he got sick so I'm a last-minute fill-in."

She rested a hand on his arm. "I'm happy I ran into you."

She smiled warmly and sounded so genuinely pleased that Dan found himself relaxing for the first time since he'd walked into the ballroom. He'd been lonely since Amy left and it was nice to see a friendly face.

"Care to dance?" he asked impulsively. If he was forced to

spend the evening mingling he might as well try to have a good time.

Bree's smile widened. "I thought you'd never ask."

"Are you still dating Jake?" Dan had been so furious with Jake —and with himself—that he hadn't seen much of the man during the past month.

"Good Lord, no." Bree laughed as if he'd made a joke. "We never did date. I just went to that one party with him. I've been seeing someone else. We just broke up."

She paused and cast him a speculative gaze. "I heard Amy moved out."

"Yes, she did." Thankfully they'd reached the dance floor and instead of saying more, Dan took Bree into his arms.

As she cuddled up against him, he realized she smelled as good as she looked. Dan inhaled the light citrus scent and let his hand caress the soft silky skin of her back.

He waited. Waited to feel a jolt of lust. Waited to experience the urge to pull her close. Waited for that rush of desire that would make him want to kiss her.

Instead he felt...nothing. If it were Amy, he'd be already kissing her and thinking of ways to ditch the party so he could get her back home and into his bed.

"...you might be interested."

Dan lifted his gaze and blinked. "Interested?"

"In a kitten," Bree said, a hint of exasperation in her tone. "Like I was saying, Kellycat, my Scottish Fold, had kittens six weeks ago and I'm looking for good homes."

"A cat is the last thing I want or need," Dan said absently. He wondered if Amy was going to be going home with Steven tonight. His hand clenched into a fist behind Bree's back.

"I was thinking of Emma," Bree said, a note of concern in her voice. "She lost her mother and now Amy. I was an only child and I know how lonely it can be."

Dan resisted the urge to tell her to mind her own business but reminded himself that Bree was only being a concerned friend.

"Emma's not lonely," Dan said firmly through gritted teeth, hoping Bree would get the message and let the subject drop. "She's always had lots of friends."

"Friends are fine." Bree laid her head against his chest. "But they can't cuddle with you. We all need someone to hold. Someone to love."

Dan's heart clenched as an image of Amy flitted across his consciousness. He'd had a best friend, someone to hold, someone to—

"I've got the prettiest black-and-white," Bree said. "Very nice markings."

Dan had finally had enough. "I don't like cats. I won't have one in my house."

Dan didn't know if it was his tone of voice or his flat dismissal of the feline species that raised Bree's ire. Her blue eyes flashed and she went rigid in his arms.

"Emma loves kittens." Bree lifted her chin. "You won't even consider getting her one."

"That's right." He breathed a sigh of relief. Finally he'd gotten through to her. "No cats."

"Because you say so."

"Yes, because I say so." Dan wondered where this belligerence was coming from. He'd dated Bree for months and had never seen this side of her.

She huffed out a breath. "You haven't changed. Not one bit."

Dan had a feeling he shouldn't ask but he couldn't help himself. "What are you talking about?"

"You want to know why we didn't work out?" There it was again, that argumentative tone. He almost wished he was back under the mistletoe worrying about the city official's wife. He decided to play along. After all, the question was a no-brainer.

They'd broken up because she'd wanted a more serious relationship. He didn't.

"Okay, Bree," he said. "Tell me. Why didn't we work out?"

"Because of your pigheadedness." Her blue eyes narrowed. "I'm sick of men who get mired in the past and refuse to move on."

Dan wasn't sure what had set Bree off, but he sensed she was just getting started. "I—"

"I, I, I," she snapped. "What? *I* can't let myself love you because I'm still in love with my dead wife?"

"Bree," he said in a low warning tone.

"At least be honest with yourself." Bree's voice trembled with emotion. "You're afraid to love again, afraid of getting hurt."

"You don't have any idea what it's like to lose a spouse."

"No, and I don't have any idea what it's like to get divorced, either. But I know when someone is letting the past screw up their future."

"Divorce?" Dan asked, now thoroughly confused.

Bree waved a dismissive hand. "A guy I'd been dating went through a bitter divorce. The problem is he's still letting his ex-wife's betrayal color his view of all women."

Now, Dan understood. Bree had really liked the guy. Once again things hadn't worked out for her.

"You'll find someone else."

"What about you?" Bree asked. "Will you find a woman to replace Amy?"

Dan stiffened. He didn't want to talk about Amy. Not with Bree. Not with anyone. "I have a temporary nanny."

"That's not what I'm talking about." Bree's eyes darkened. "You two were close. Now she's gone."

"She accepted a full-time chef position at Chez Gladines," Dan informed Bree. "Amy had to make a choice."

"Emma's in school all day." Bree waved that away. "You could have worked something out. You weren't willing to work with her. It's all or nothing with you. Just like with Emma and the cat."

"You think you know so much." Dan's temper had reached the breaking point. "I don't see *you* doing all that great in your personal life."

Bree's cheeks reddened as if she'd been slapped but her gaze remained steady and her chin up. "At least I'm open to love. When I find the right one, I'm not going to be rigid and insist on everything being my way. I'll look for ways to make it work."

"With that accommodating attitude I'm surprised you're still not with your divorced friend," Dan said, his tone slightly mocking.

"It takes two to make things work, Dan." Bree met his gaze. "Kyle wasn't ready or able to get past his fear. The problem is once he is, I won't be around."

Dan shifted uncomfortably from one foot to another.

Bree's expression softened. "I know you really cared for Amy. I saw the way the two of you were together. Do you know that when we dated, I was jealous of her?"

Dan frowned. "Of Amy?"

"Yes, of Amy." Bree chuckled then sobered. "There was a chemistry between you two, a closeness that went far beyond friendship. When you'd talk about her, you'd get this look in your eye. Sometimes I had the feeling I was dating a married man."

Dan swallowed hard against the sudden lump in his throat. Even if he could respond, he didn't know what to say. There *had* been something special between him and Amy.

"You care for her. As your friend, I just want you to take a look at what you're losing. For what? Because you can't let go of the past?"

"You make it sound so easy," Dan said. "Tess was my wife. I'd loved her since we were kids in school. She—"

"She's dead, Dan." Bree's tone was flat but not without

compassion. "She'd want you to move on with your life. Fall in love again."

"I don't know if I can..."

"I think you already have." Bree's lips curved. "Now you just have to decide what you're going to do about it."

CHAPTER NINETEEN

Amy leaned her cheek against Steven's chest and let the music wash over her, grateful she could enjoy the closeness without worrying her actions would be misconstrued.

When she'd made the break with Dan, Steven had seen the split as an opportunity to deepen their relationship. He'd been stunned when she'd told him she thought of him only as a friend. In the end he'd appreciated her honesty. When his date had canceled at the last minute, he'd called and asked her to accompany him to the Mayor's Ball...as a friend.

She hadn't really wanted to go but she'd decided a night out might do her some good. She'd been in a funk for a few weeks. Some of it was living with Verna.

Her aunt had run her household a certain way for many years and having Amy around disrupted her schedule.

Some of it was her new job. While she was up to the challenge and learned something new every day, she missed being her own boss. She liked the flexibility she'd had being a nanny and doing small catering jobs on the side.

Most of her blue mood she knew could be directly tied to Dan Major. Her anger over his deception had diminished to a profound regret. If he'd had concerns about Emma's welfare, they could have talked about it, strategized. But to deliberately set out to make her fall in love with him...to deliberately seduce her... well, she'd expected better of him.

She knew he liked her. She had no doubt that he wanted her. Even now, when she picked Emma up she'd catch him looking at her and the longing in his eyes would take her breath away. Yes, he wanted her. He just didn't *love* her.

Tears momentarily blurred her vision. Amy blinked rapidly for several seconds until she could see clearly again.

"All this dancing is making me thirsty." Steven slowed his steps. "How about we get some champagne and go for a stroll?"

They'd reached the edge of the dance floor when Amy stopped in her tracks. For a moment she felt light-headed.

"Dan." Her gaze widened to include the woman standing next to him, a proprietary arm through his. "Bree. What a surprise."

The introductions went quickly. Bree's eyes brightened with interest when she heard Steven's name.

"Bree is an attorney, too, Steven," Amy added. "She works for Seim Anderson."

Steven's expression brightened. "I met Jerry Seim my first day in Chicago."

The comment started an animated conversation between the two lawyers, leaving Amy and Dan standing at the sidelines.

She gazed at Dan, her heart in her throat. She'd never known a man who looked so good in a tux— although she did notice his tie needed straightening. For once she kept her fingers to herself.

"Would you care to dance?" Dan asked politely.

Amy said neither yes or no, but let him take her hand and lead her back onto the dance floor. The familiar scent of his cologne sent her senses into overdrive and the light touch of his hand made her pulse pound.

When Dan placed a hand on her waist and drew her close, and with his other hand took hers in a warm clasp and began to move her in time to the music, Amy was unprepared for the intimacy of it.

"You're gorgeous," he whispered.

Amy's face warmed. She closed her eyes, trying to concentrate on the music, or the conversations surrounding them, on anything except how good his body felt pressed against hers.

"You're the most beautiful woman in the room."

She kept her eyes tightly closed and acted as if she hadn't heard.

Dan couldn't believe after four long weeks she was finally back in his arms where she belonged.

"I've missed you," Dan said, embarrassed at the breathless quality of his voice. Oddly enough, he felt breathless.

The minute he'd touched her, he wanted nothing more than to take her home, lie naked beside her and touch her everywhere. He'd start with her breasts...

"Are you and Bree seeing each other again?" Amy tilted her head and gazed up at him.

Her words had the dousing effect of ice water, and the dream vanished.

"No, we're not. I ran into her just a few minutes before I saw you." He cleared his throat. "How about you and Steven? Are you exclusive?"

Amy shook her head. "We're just friends."

Relief rushed through him. When he'd seen them together...

"Anything new with Bree?"

The question took him by surprise. Until he felt Amy's hand tremble and realized she was nervous and merely making light conversation.

"Not really." He chuckled. "Unless you count the fact that her Scotland cat just had kittens."

Scotland cat? It didn't sound right, but he must have been close enough to be understood because Amy's eyes brightened. "Kellycat's a momma?"

"She had a whole bunch of kittens and apparently they're ready to be adopted." Dan couldn't believe he was having a conversation about *cats*. But he'd talk about them all night long if it would keep Amy in his arms.

"I'd love to see them." Amy's smile brightened then faded. "On second thought, I'd better not."

"Why not?" Dan tightened his arms around her. Dancing with her was heaven. Absolute paradise. There was no space between them, no way they could get any closer—at least not with their clothes on. He'd missed her so much...

"I'd want to take one home." Her voice sounded sad and wistful.

Dan opened his mouth then shut it. The last thing he wanted to do during this brief time together was hear himself talk.

"Didn't you used to have a cat?" Dan asked, moving his hand slowly down the bare skin exposed by the deep V of the back of her dress.

She quivered and his body responded immediately. But if she could feel his arousal, she gave no indication.

"Yes," she murmured. "His name was Mittens and he was black and white and very beautiful. My father got him for me as a birthday present. When I went to live with my aunt, he had to go to the animal shelter. I'm sure someone nice adopted him."

Though her tone didn't vary, Dan knew her so well he heard the pain beneath the matter-of-fact words.

"Losing him had to have been hard," he said.

Amy's eyes took on a distant faraway look. "I promised myself that when I grew up and had a place of my own I'd get another Scottish Fold—that's the kind of cat Mittens was—but I've never lived anywhere that's allowed pets."

Dan had known she liked cats but he realized with sudden insight that if they'd married she'd still not have one. The knowledge filled him with shame. Too late, he realized he'd give Amy the sun and the moon if he could. Hell, he'd even give her a cat.

He stopped, startled. He'd never go to that extreme for someone he just liked. Only for someone he *loved*.

Was Bree right? Had he told himself he couldn't love anyone but Tess because he was *afraid?*

It hardly seemed possible. After all, he'd never been a man to make decisions based on fear. But if he didn't love Amy, why had he been so miserable without her? He'd tried to tell himself it was because he and Emma had grown to depend on her.

Her replacement did a wonderful job taking care of things around the house so it couldn't be that. It was Amy he missed. Amy who made the house a home.

I'm in love with Amy.

The words echoed through his head and he knew, without a doubt that they were true. With Tess, love had hit him like a lightning bolt. With Amy, love had come softly. It had crept into his heart and taken up residence without him even being aware it had happened.

Now, all he had to do was to let Amy know how he felt...and hope it wasn't too late.

~

"Emma." Amy opened the door and called out. She'd tried the doorbell but no one came. It was the Sunday before Christmas and she and Emma were going to the mall.

The house was strangely silent. Sunday was Marjorie's day off so she hadn't expected to see the housekeeper. She had expected to find Dan and Emma at home, especially since she'd just confirmed the five o'clock pickup time with Dan earlier that afternoon.

The call had been the first time they'd talked since the party. She'd worried it might be awkward but Dan had been in good spirits—asking her about her job and seeming genuinely pleased when she reported things were going well.

Maintaining a positive relationship was a good thing, she told herself. It was important for Emma that they be cordial. Wednesday night had gone a little beyond cordial. For a moment on the dance floor Amy had felt as if Dan might try to kiss her. Even worse, the way her body had been responding to his closeness, she had the feeling she'd have let him.

When she and Dan had returned to Steven and Bree, the two attorneys were seated alone at a large round table totally engrossed in a conversation about some legal case.

Dan hadn't seemed to mind. He'd confiscated glasses of champagne from a passing waiter and pulled out a couple of chairs across the table from Bree and Steven.

Amy had been surprised when Dan brought up her job at Chez Gladines. It was the first time she'd discussed the position with him and, looking back, she was sure she'd bored him with way too many details. Sitting with him at that linen clad table had reminded her of all the times they'd talked over breakfast, all the discussions they'd had at the supper table.

It would be so easy to be drawn into the trap of equating interest with love. She'd made that mistake once and she wasn't going down that road again.

"Emma," Amy called again, glancing at her watch. "We need to go. The mall closes early today."

Still no answer.

Amy left the kitchen and headed for the parlor, where Emma loved to sit and read. But she only got as far as the dining room before she stopped. Though there was no food yet on the table, there was crystal and china and candles. A fresh flower centerpiece.

Spider mums. Her favorite.

Amy's heart twisted.

It didn't take a genius to know that Dan had a romantic evening for two planned. Either he'd gotten back with Bree or there was someone new in his life. She wondered if he'd deliberately planned this date knowing Emma would be gone most of the evening? It wasn't any of her business, of course. She was simply curious.

"The brisket is in the oven."

Amy jumped at the sound of the voice and turned to find Dan in the doorway.

"It smells delicious," she said. "Brisket has always been one of my favorites."

It was a stupid thing to say and Amy regretted the comment the second it left her lips. After all, what did it matter what *she* liked. *She* wasn't the one who'd be eating it.

She swallowed hard past the sudden lump in her throat. "Is Emma upstairs?"

"Actually—" Dan shoved his hands into his pockets and rocked back on his heels "—there's been a slight change in plans. Emma is spending the night at Rehn's."

Amy's heart fell. "She was going to buy your Christmas gift tonight. I can't believe she forgot."

Emma had been excited about this day for weeks. Yet, she'd decided to spend the night with a neighbor? It didn't make sense.

"She didn't forget." A rueful smile tipped Dan's lips. "The only way I could get her to go to Rehn's was to tell her you and I had plans for the evening."

Amy stiffened. She couldn't believe he'd lied to his daughter so that he could get together with his new girlfriend. "That's not fair, Dan. You shouldn't get her hopes up just because you want to spend an evening with—"

"With you," he said, finishing the sentence. "I want to spend the evening with you. There's so much I have to say."

Amy glanced at the table. It had seduction written all over it. Okay, so he was lonely. He probably missed having her in his bed. Goodness knows she'd missed holding him tight. But as much as she'd like to share that intimacy again, the physical closeness was no longer enough.

"I don't think that'd be a good idea." Amy's fingers tightened around her purse. "What more is there to say? Everything's already been said."

Dan swallowed hard and took a step forward.

"I haven't said I love you before," he said softly. "I do. Very much."

He was surprised, once the words were out, that he should feel so unmanned, and that tears should be stinging his eyes.

When she just kept staring at him, he turned away and continued.

"I know I haven't been good to you." He shook his head. "I've been selfish. I only thought about myself."

"That's not true." A tiny catch sounded in her voice.

"It is. When I think back on it now, I'm so ashamed. I wish I could tell you how much I regret the way I treated you, as if you were just an employee."

"Dan," she said firmly. "I *was* your employee. If anyone was at fault it was me for foolishly believing that I was different, that you could love me."

He felt her hand on his arm.

"You were good to me. You made me feel like a part of the family. That said, it was wrong of you to lead me on."

"I love you," Dan said.

"No." She shook her head. "You love Tess. She's the only woman you'll ever love."

"I love you," he repeated emphatically.

"You don't," she insisted. "You told me over and over again that Tess is the only woman you'll ever love."

"I did love Tess," he admitted, "but I love you, too."

"Dan," Amy said patiently as if speaking to a child. "I understand you need a mother for Emma and someone to take care of you and your house, but lying isn't the answer."

Amy turned to go but Dan grabbed her arm and pulled her to him, hugging her tightly.

"I was such a fool," he murmured. "I know I hurt you. Listen to me, please. I won't deny that I loved Tess. I won't deny it because I did. What I didn't realize is that I've been afraid. I didn't understand anything about love. I thought I could decide my feelings—thought I could decide whether to love someone or not—but that isn't how love works. It happens all on its own. I kept telling myself that I couldn't love you, that I *didn't* love you, but I did."

Amy wanted to believe him. More than anything she wanted to believe his words.

"What about my career?" she asked.

"That's another thing I regret," Dan said. "I just assumed you'd want to build on our family right away. I didn't even ask what you wanted. I think I was afraid if you had a career, our home life would come in a distant second like it did with Tess."

"I'd never let that happen," Amy said. "You and Emma would always be the priority."

"I realize that now. I know we can make it work," he murmured against her hair. "Just give me another chance. I'll show you how much I love you."

Amy wanted to believe him. But she couldn't forget his conversation with Jake. "How do I know you're not just saying this because you need a mother for Emma? Because you're afraid of Gwen and Phil getting her if something happens to you?"

Her words made Dan's heart ache with remorse and sorrow.

"I spoke with my attorney and he said they could fight all they want but the courts would uphold my wishes. I also spoke with Gwen and Phil and made it clear that I wanted you to raise Emma." Dan's lips lifted in a rueful smile. "It was never an issue. I just thought it would be."

Amy's brows pulled together. "Why didn't you check this out before?"

"I know it was stupid," Dan said, a sheepish look on his face. "The only explanation I've been able to come up with is that it gave me a reason to marry you without admitting to myself that I loved you."

Dan laced his fingers through her hair. "I'm not asking you to be my wife because I *need* to marry you. I *want* to marry you. I love you."

An ache of longing raged through Amy. She closed her eyes and let her head rest against his chest. Would she be making a mistake by saying yes?

"Mew."

Amy's eyelids popped open. She shifted in Dan's arms just in time to see a small furry head peer around the corner.

"What's that?"

Dan smiled. "Your Christmas present. From me to you with all my love."

He reached down and scooped the black and white kitten into his arms. "She's a Scottish Fold. See how her ears flop over. Her eyes are more round than oval."

Amy's heart melted. Tears filled her eyes. "You don't like cats."

"You do," he said. "That's what matters."

She took the kitten from his arms and held it tight against her. "She even has four white feet, just like Mittens."

"I'll make you happy, Amy," Dan said. "Just give me the chance."

He appeared relaxed but she could see the tenseness in the set of his shoulders, in the tiny muscle that jumped in his jaw.

Amy leaned over and dropped the ball of fluff gently to the floor. While she loved her new kitten, she loved Dan more. Right now he needed her attention and reassurance.

"I love you, Dan," she said very softly, "and I know you love me."

He grabbed her, held her fast. "Thank you, God." His voice was thick with emotion, with relief. He kissed her again, this time so fiercely they almost tumbled into the table. He kept kissing her.

"Will you marry me, Amy? Will you be my wife?"

She lifted a finger to her lips and pretended to think, but inside her heart had already started to sing.

"Say yes," he said, kissing her. "Come on. Say yes."

When she didn't answer, he kissed her again, then again.

"Say yes," he whispered against her lips.

"Mew."

Tiny little claws dug into Amy's ankle. She yelped and jerked back from Dan's arms.

Dan's brows pulled together. His gaze dropped to the black and white kitten that now sat staring up at them. After a moment his frown eased. His lips twitched. He grinned.

"See," he said finally. "Even the cat thinks you should give me a chance."

Amy could only laugh.

"I love you, Amy," Dan said, taking her hands, his grin fading, his expression turning serious. "If you marry me, I'll spend the rest of my life making you happy."

Of that, Amy now had no doubt.

"Yes," she said, nodding her head emphatically.

"Yes, you know I'll spend the rest of my life making you happy?" he asked cautiously. "Or yes, you'll marry me?"

Amy's heart overflowed with joy. She placed her hands on his shoulders and kissed him full on the mouth. "Yes, to both questions."

As Dan pulled her close murmuring words of love, Amy knew the fairy-tale ending was finally hers.

A man to love.

A child to cherish.

A cat to litter train.

It was all she'd ever wanted and more.

~

Dan was already downstairs when Amy woke the next morning. She stared down at the sparkling diamond on her left hand. Today, they'd get their marriage license. Tomorrow would be their wedding day.

Just in time for Christmas.

She would be his Christmas present and he would be hers. Dan had told her last night that having her as his wife was the only gift he wanted. Then he'd proceeded to show her again just how much she was loved.

Amy showered and dressed quickly, happiness bubbling up inside her. She gave the kitten a quick pat and a treat but didn't linger. She wanted to be downstairs before Emma got home so that she and Dan could tell her the good news together.

She was outside the kitchen when she heard Emma talking to Dan. Amy paused to listen, her heart in her throat.

"Did Amy come over last night, Daddy?"

"Yes, she did."

"Did you two kiss and make up?"

Dan's cough sounded suspiciously like laughter. "Yes, we did."

Amy's skin warmed, remembering just how thoroughly they'd kissed and made up.

"Is Amy coming home today?" The childish hope in Emma's voice tore at Amy's heartstrings.

She couldn't bear to wait a second longer. Before Dan could answer Amy stepped around the corner. "I'm already here."

Emma squealed and ran into Amy's open arms, pressing her tiny body tight against her. After a moment, she lifted her head, her gaze anxiously searching Amy's. "How long are you staying?"

Amy lifted her gaze to meet Dan's, the promise in his eyes a reflection of what was in her heart. She smiled down at Emma. "Forever."

From Cindy Kirk

Thanks for spending time with Dan and Amy. I empathized with Amy. I can't imagine how difficult it would be to work for a man you loved who didn't appear to feel the same way about you. There were times I wanted to scream "You have the perfect woman right under your roof, Dan!" Dan had a lot of growing to do before he could be the kind of man Amy deserved. I'm glad you came along for that journey.

If you love uplifting romance, you're going to LOVE Her Ten-Year Secret. It's one of those books that will tug at your heartstrings and keep you reading WAY too late at night. Fans of heartwarming romance rave about this book and I know you will too.

Dive into this amazing story now <u>Her Ten-Year Secret</u> (or turn the page for a sneak peek)

SNEAK PEEK OF HER TEN-YEAR SECRET

"Patty Bradley? Is that you?"

Trish's fingers clenched the stem of the crystal goblet. It had been ten years since she'd heard that voice, but she recognized it immediately.

Ignoring a momentary impulse to run, Trish took a leisurely sip of wine and turned. "Why, Jack Krieger, what a surprise."

Five years in public relations had served Trish well. Strong and steady, her voice gave no indication of the sudden tightness that gripped her chest at the sight of him.

"I hardly recognized you." Jack took a step back and stared, his gaze openly admiring. "You look wonderful."

"You don't look so bad yourself," Trish said, keeping her tone light and offhand.

All these years she'd told herself that he wasn't really as attractive as she'd remembered. She was wrong.

The toffee-colored hair of his youth had deepened to a warm chestnut and his vivid blue eyes, once the color of the sky on a clear summer day, now glowed like dark sapphires. Age had only added depth and maturity to the boyish features she remembered so well. If Jack had been handsome at eighteen, he was devastating at twenty-eight.

Life had obviously been good to him. His smile was genuine and he wore the easy self-assurance of someone who knows his place in the world.

She should hate him. His lies and deceit had taken the last of her innocence. But it wasn't easy for Trish to hate anyone, much less Jack Krieger. Still, she was no fool. She'd never forget how he'd used her.

Trish hardened her gaze.

Jack took a sip of his wine and smiled, apparently not noticing.

"I can't believe how you've changed," he said with a flash of perfect white teeth. "You look terrific."

"Thanks." Trish accepted the compliment graciously. Even she, who'd never been all that confident about her appearance, had to admit that tonight Jack was right. She looked fabulous. She'd taken extra time with her makeup and dressed with special care, trying to bolster a flagging confidence that had been seriously shaken by the recent unexpected loss of her job.

She knew his admiring look had less to do with her makeup and clothes and more to do with the svelte figure beneath the silk sheath. In his mind he was seeing the girl she'd been in high school, the girl that had been good enough to sleep with in secret but not good enough to be his girlfriend in public. His dowdy next-door neighbor, the one kids loved to tease. He was remembering Fatty Patty.

Fatty Patty.

Trish forced a deep breath and released it. How the horrid name still hurt. Even years and distance and success hadn't been able to completely erase the memories of her classmates' cruel taunts.

That was ten years ago, and she'd come a long way since those days.

"I never thought I'd see you again," Jack said finally. "After graduation it was like you'd dropped off the face of the earth."

"I hardly think Washington is off the face of the earth," she said lightly.

"It might as well be." He shot her a penetrating stare. "No one knew where you were. You never even wrote."

Trish smiled and forced a shoulder up in a careless shrug as if cutting all ties with Lynnwood had been of no consequence. In truth, it had been the first of many difficult decisions she'd had to make.

"Honey, aren't you going to introduce me?" Pete Minchow, Trish's escort for the evening, took the momentary silence as an invitation to join in.

"Pete, I don't think—"

"I don't believe we've met." Without missing a beat, Jack extended his hand to the other man. "I'm Jack Krieger, an old friend of Patty's from high school."

It was all Trish could do not to groan out loud. There he went again, pulling in the past along with that ridiculous name. Somehow it didn't sound so ridiculous when he said it. It never had.

"Pete Minchow." Pete shook Jack's hand as if he was priming a pump. Originally from Texas, the man had the good-ol'-boy image down to a science and used it to his advantage in his business dealings. But Trish knew that beneath that country boy exterior beat the heart of a shrewd businessman. "Pleased to meet you. Any friend of Trish here is a friend of mine."

"Trish?" Jack's brows drew together in a frown. "What happened to Patty?"

Pete gazed at Trish for a moment. "Patty, eh? I kinda like it."

"Well, I don't." Trish plucked a piece of lint from the collar of Pete's tux. "And if you ever call me that, you're a dead man."

She smiled and took a sip of her wine.

Pete's eyes widened for a second, then he chuckled with good-natured humor. "I'll have to remember that."

"Do you work for the government, Pete?" Jack tilted his head questioningly as if he was really interested in what Pete had to say. It was the same look he used to give her when they'd sit on her porch swing and she'd tell him about her day.

Her heart twisted at the memory.

"Pete owns his own business." Trish looked up at the lean, tall Texan suddenly grateful to have such a handsome man at her side. "He's not into politics. Or playing games."

Jack cocked his head and studied Trish for a moment before turning his attention back to Pete. "I thought everybody in this town had something to do with politics."

"Lord, no," Pete said with a laugh. "I'm into cars. New, used, buy, sell, lease, you name it, and I've got 'em. We're one of the largest GM dealers on the eastern seaboard."

"Really?" Jack said. "Impressive."

Although the words sounded sincere, Trish had to wonder. They were, after all, living and working in a town where you ate, slept and breathed politics. Few would find owning a car dealership impressive.

"Have you and Patty been dating long?" Jack asked.

"Don't you mean *Trish?*" Pete gave Trish a wink and took a sip of wine. "What's it been darlin'? Five? Six months?"

"Something like that," she said, grateful Pete was keeping his mouth shut about the nature of their relationship. They were merely friends with an understanding. She accompanied him to an occasional party if he needed an escort and he did the same for her.

It was the need to network that had caused Trish to forgo popcorn and a movie with Tommy and accept Pete's invitation to one of the hottest parties in D.C. The event was the perfect opportunity to make contacts and get some leads on a new position.

It had been two months since she'd been restructured out of her dream job with one of the top PR firms in Washington. Corporate downsizing they'd called it. All she knew was that once her savings ran out, the wolves would be at the door. Anxiety nipped at her, but Trish had been through worse times and survived. Even if only one of her prayers were answered, she'd be okay.

"She took back her maiden name after they split. That's been what? Six or seven years?" Pete turned toward Trish with an expectant look.

"A long time," Trish said.

Pete had obviously been repeating the same lies she'd been telling everyone for years: that she'd married out of high school and divorced shortly after. It was a little fabrication that easily explained the presence of a now-nine-year-old son and no husband.

"You're divorced?" Jack blurted out, his eyes wide with surprise. "Your grandmother never even told me you'd married."

"Then I bet she never told you Trish has a son, either?" Pete said.

It was all Trish could do not to give him a swift jab in the ribs. Would Pete ever learn to keep his mouth shut?

"From my," Trish raised her chin with a cool stare in Jack's direction, "first marriage."

"First marriage?" The muscle in Jack's jaw jumped. "You've been married more than once?"

She'd never been married, never planned to marry. But that was her business, certainly not his.

"Sometimes life doesn't work out the way we want." Trish lowered her voice, being purposefully mysterious. But the words hit too close to home, and her tone turned sharp. "Not that it's any of your business."

"Now, darlin'. I know you're just having some fun, but the man thinks you're serious." Pete put his arm around her and gave her a big squeeze. "Jack, I've known Trish for quite a few years and, as far as I know, she's only been married once."

"So you have a little boy," Jack mused.

"Tommy's a cute kid," Pete said, when Trish didn't respond. "He's not all that little anymore."

"How old is your son?" Jack's gaze shifted to Trish.

Trish thought quickly. Had she mentioned to Pete that Tommy had recently turned nine? Even if she had, would he remember?

"He's eight." She lifted the glass of merlot to her lips and took a sip.

"That old?" His brows drew together. She could almost see the wheels turning in his head. "You must have gotten pregnant—"

"About a year after I left Lynnwood. That next spring." Trish said, chopping a whole year off Tommy's age. Thankfully, Jack would never see the boy. Tall for his age, Tommy could more easily pass for ten than eight.

"Were you living in D.C. then?"

The question was probably completely innocent, considering they hadn't seen each other for so long, but the more she talked the more likely she was to trip herself up.

"That was so long ago." Trish waved one hand carelessly.

"Do you ever miss Lynnwood?" Jack's gaze never left her face.

"Not really." She drained the last of her wine from the glass. "There's nothing for me there."

"There's friends and fam—" Jack stopped suddenly. She knew he was remembering that her grandmother had been her only relative and that she'd died earlier in the year. "Well, what about friends? Don't you miss them?"

"Oh, puh-leeze." Trish rolled her eyes. "We both know I was hardly Miss Popular. I don't think I had any friends back then."

"Yes, you did," Jack said.

She quirked an eyebrow questioningly.

"You had me," Jack said softly. "I was your friend."

Trish lifted her chin and met his gaze, willing him to see in her eyes what she couldn't, wouldn't say in Pete's presence. That a friend never would have done what he did to her.

"Where in the heck is this Lindwood place anyway?" Pete munched thoughtfully on a tiny wafer topped with salmon, seemingly oblivious to the electricity crackling in the air.

"Actually, it's Lynnwood," Jack said, slanting a glance at Trish. "It's a small town in Kansas, about twenty miles northwest of Kansas City. Patty, uh, I mean Trish, and I grew up there."

"I love those little bumps in the road." Pete washed down the salmon with the last of his wine. "Sometimes I think about moving back to Texas, to my hometown. Then I remember that I've got more cars on my lot than there are people in that godforsaken place and the urge passes."

He laughed and grabbed another drink from a passing waiter. "Tell me Jack, do you still live in Lindwood?"

This time Jack didn't bother to correct him.

"Lynnwood is still home," Jack said, glancing at Trish. "Right now I'm living in Arlington."

A chill traveled up Trish's spine. She and Tommy lived in Vienna, only a few metro stops away.

"Great. You have a business card on you?" Pete smiled. "I'll give you a call and maybe we can all get together sometime."

"I'd like that." Jack reached into his pocket. He pulled out a silver holder, extracted a card and scribbled some numbers on it before handing it to Pete. "Lunch usually works for me."

"Wonderful." Pete grabbed the card and shoved it into his pocket. "Tell me, have you ever been to that little Greek place over by Dupont Circle?"

Jack paused for a moment, then shook his head.

"Let me tell you it may look like a dump, but their food is the best. You'll love it."

"I'm sure I will," Jack said. His gaze shifted to Trish.

She forced a smile. As far as she was concerned, Pete could circular file Jack's business card the second he got home.

Because there was one thing she knew for sure...it would be a cold day in hell before she'd willingly have anything to do with Jack Krieger again.

Eager to dive into the rest of the story? Click here to read Her Ten-Year Secret

Made in the USA
Las Vegas, NV
02 August 2022